The Chosen One to Die

The Fallen

ISBN: 9781795597418

Original title: El Elegido para Morir

Cover illustration by: Sandro Sánches

Translation by: Gabriela Velasco

Everyone who helped me to jump

You made this possible.

Index

Prologue

First part: «His Yellow Eyes»

Chapter 1: «When the Night Was Red»

Chapter 2: «The Eyes of a Murderer»

Chapter 3: «Two Black Wells»

Chapter 4: «Assault Plans»

Chapter 5: «Death Wound»

Chapter 6: «New People, New Blood»

Chapter 7: «Fresh Blood»

Chapter 8: «The Titans' True Appearance»

Chapter 9: «Entrance to the Submerged City»

Part Two: «An Appointment in the Other World, that World in Which they Only Talk about Death»

Chapter 10: «Hecate's Descendants»

Chapter 11: «If it Is for Love... »

Chapter 12: «The Brightness of Memories»

Chapter 13: «Black Soul, Black Hand»

Epilogue: «The Worst Nightmare»

Acknowledgements

Prologue

They do not eat when they are hungry; they do not drink when they are thirsty; and they feel neither the cold nor the heat. Their eyes, which are two bright dots at night, do not close when the wind gets infuriated. Fatigue does not make a dent in their vigorous bodies of iron, even when the mud makes it difficult to move towards a new prey.

The rain, which hides the sound of the hunter's footsteps, will conceal amidst the ground, the cries of an unwary hiker.

In the darkness there is not only silence, there are also beings who crave the smell of an open throat.

Part 1:

«His Yellow Eyes»

Chapter 1

«When the Night Was Red»

It's always the others who die. But now that she has given me the gold sparkle, I know I've always been her chosen one. I was her light, her guide and hope... Although I know that she is comforted with knowing that, I was always the second part of her sleepless nights...

Fragment of Hecate's lost diary.

That night the moon shone as if it took it just a few moments to reflect the light. Feeling its rays on my face, made me smile. For the first time in a very long time, we felt free. I could no longer remember how much my body had been broken, yearning to recover the necessary strength to break those chains which, at that very moment, would be tinkling some sinister melody in the shadows.

We ran through the woods, jumping over the fragile branches that were splitting under our weight. The soft caress of the air, removing our golden hair, brought to my chest a green leaf, which gave off a stench that we remembered very well. We formed a dense yellow layer and although concealed in the shadows, it gave shelter to the nocturnal animals, which despite of not having seen each other since they had banished us, they would recognize us. With a distant howl, began our first day of fighting for the land that belonged to us.

A few meters ahead of me, the strongest member of the community, who at the time, was my father, led the way. I turned my head and seeing that we were all a gigantic unit that almost felt the same, I knew that all the crimes that humanity owed to us, they would pay in the coming nights. The light of the night struck squarely my father's back, which gave him a whitish appearance, which made his traits even sharper. The long yellow mane framed his face, and his blue eyes shone like two lights at night. I jumped on the branch next to him. What appeared before our eyes, in that clearing of the forest, caused all the hatred within us to ooze hard.

"Father," I said. And I added in a whisper laden with the most primitive of the furies: "Humans."

He smiled with his eyes closed, which seemed to turn off part of the light that brightened the night. There were few drops of water on our bodies, we were practically dry. The muscles of my body were tense to see these creatures so close. After having hated them for so much time to see them lying there, without even noticing our presence, I wondered what kind of creatures their ancestors were, who had managed to defeat us; but above all, what kind of creatures we were.

"Let it be me who comes first." I asked. Yearning to have the privilege of being the first to shed their blood in the sweet ground.

He agreed. It was going to be an honor and after all, being the two strongest members of the community granted us certain privileges in front of others.

I let myself fall without making any noise, the print of my landing was etched on the ground. Walking as they did seem strange to me at first, it almost seemed awkward. The humans in the forest were a group of ten. Five of them had retired to sleep and the others continued to speak and laugh in the light of the bonfire. Soon they would end their laughter, I thought. There were three women and two men. They all had black hair and tanned skin. I walked, slowly, trying to control the movements to look like a human in distress. I wanted to play.

Alarmed to see me, one of the women did not hesitate to approach running with a blanket to cover my body. The others, paralyzed without knowing what they were supposed to do, were put in motion when they saw the other human concerned. They were trying to call someone to help us. I listened to their rampant hearts as they were facing the situation that had been presented to them so suddenly. They believed they would have a simple summer night and not everything that was coming on. They woke up the others, who immediately armed themselves, believing that I had been attacked by an animal they could hunt.

That woman offered me water and food. I looked at her in depth, trying to glimpse something of value inside; but all I saw was a void, that looked back at me. I no longer remember her face, like the many others... of all that came along after I killed her; they've all been diluted in my memory. She thought that I didn't understand her language and really tried hard to communicate with me. That girl stayed by my side, while the others were looking for something that could put an end to the situation. I watched the frenzy of the group. Their numerous belongings scattered along the place which, not long ago, only lodged laughter; the objects they used to sleep; their weapons, loaded to fire against... against what? They didn't even know what was happening. But there was one of them that did not move; one who did nothing different to look at me with the most absolute terror painted on his face. He dropped a white book to the ground, which ricocheted and by few centimeters did not fall into the bonfire. His knees hit the ground as the tears spurted out of his eyes. He had noticed. And I couldn't wait any longer!

My group was already around the camp. I wondered if that boy would see them the same way I did. I looked for the last time to the female human and in her eyes I did not find anything different from the stain of the sub-race; the stain of the traitors, who dared to banish us from our own home. I went through her chest with my arm; it was like putting half a body in water that's about to freeze. Her heart fit into my palm; from his lips arose a supplication, before falling dead at my feet. As if she hadn't even realized it was too late. What remained steadfast in my memory, was the sad expression of her eyes as she realized that I had betrayed her, noticing the fatal mistake she had committed in trusting on me. That was the closest they would be to understanding how we had felt after offending us for so many years locked up because of their ancestors.

The other humans began to shout; those who were armed, shot at me, but their bullets and arrows tore apart in my body and those who had nothing, simply tried to escape, but it was too late. It was too late for everyone.

The heart of that human continued to beat in my hand for a few more moments. I beheld it, disgusted. I pressed it between my fingers, until it was nothing but an inert mass that I threw to the ground.

Once they were all dead, I looked at them carefully. Their bodies were scattered all over the camp. The smell of blood was very strong, but what was calling my attention was that they had not even been able to defend themselves. Were these the same ones that had banished us? Had our power increased that much? At that time, there were many questions, but I was still not interested in knowing their answers. At that moment I only craved their death. I looked at my father, who was on the other side of the glade. I smiled and he gave me back a big smirk. His body and part of his hands were covered with blood. Despite the repulsion we felt towards them, in that first attack we did not care to get stained, soon the blood of those creatures would evaporate from our skin.

For a few moments, we were the only living beings in that glade. The only company, oblivious to everything that was happening, was the bonfire that was crackling with less force and leaving some grotesque shadows projected on the forest boundary. Suddenly, we heard a muffled cry coming from there. It was another human! He ran away from us. I threw myself in his search. It was impossible for him to hide from me, because even though the night was dark I could see him. He hid behind a large tree; his breath was faltering and he gave off a strong sweet smell. I slowed down, so that he could not hear me coming and the waiting would become more agonizing. His heart fluttered unsteadily. Oh, he had a sore ankle, so he stopped. And even if he had accepted his death, he believed that it was possible that he had some glimmer of hope.

I stepped on a branch and scratched the surface of a log with the fingernails. The human screamed and tried to flee again. But this time he simply crawled, looking back, believing to see in every shadow his end; now he had considered himself dead. He fell to the ground and began to cry. He begged of me for mercy when I jumped and landed on him. I took his face with both hands. It was just a mass of flimsy bones that cried and begged to live one more day. He stopped talking when I twisted his neck and ripped his head off.

It was so easy to kill them... A single blow was enough to eliminate several. It wasn't even necessary for us to use our power to kill them. However, it is true that a certain group found something; something that helped them to be even stronger and faster. They called themselves the Hunters and did not want to share with any of us their discovery. How much I would have liked to know back then what that really meant. Perhaps if at that time we had decided that they could not monopolize a power, that they kept only for themselves, we would not have ended this way... Maybe.

The cities of that world choked the earth and obscured the air. Little was the space which was free for nature; almost everything collapsed. In one of those grey places, I found what could be the equivalent of the Hunters' discovery: a black substance that, when coming into contact with my energy, was hardened. At first, it was just a dark stain on the floor that slowly slipped between the cracks and went up to touch my fingers. The stain adapted to me, with perfection, as if it were a fragment that I thought was lost many years ago.

We all used that material to protect ourselves and there was nothing on earth that would hold us back. Many of us wanted to end this absurd war soon, and since their weapons did not hurt us, the fact of wearing that armor made things much easier. For a long time, I wondered what had been the way in which we had been banished because, now, it did not seem that they were even close to hurt us, let alone defeat us. Their lifeless bodies, scattered everywhere, made me feel confused because, after all, they had won the first time... That event that gradually faded into my memory, concealed by the draughts, which swayed the tattered clothes of the dead.

They were so many humans... we could have been like this for decades. We decided to use our power to put an end to what would be remembered as the Great War.

I stopped for an instant on one of the burning buildings. I observed the movements of the members of the community; I heard the explosions and the shouts; and I also felt the way energy moved from one member to another. I smiled lightly, when a great explosion flooded my field of vision.

A snap produced by the armor caught my attention quickly, someone was coming.

"Daughter, why don't you fight?" Said my father, standing before me. He floated down until he laid his feet on the ground. "Are you tired already?"

His cloak fluttered around him for several moments, until it was languidly hanging on his back.

"No, Father." I pointed to the direction I was looking at, so that he would also notice. "It's just that the fire has distracted me."

That answer seemed to satisfy him. He nodded and soared in the air, returning to the battle the one I restricted myself to observe. And it was not because I was afraid or because my energy was about to run out; the reason I kept away was curiosity. It was such my desire to control the extent to which we had been strengthened that I simply believed that war with the sub-race was no longer the reason why I should be concerned, and that my new goal was to know how powerful each of us was.

I saw the Hunters, with their helmets in the shape of a bull and their big spears, throwing large beams of incandescent light against the humans, who shouted crazed when they felt the hug of the flames. I really admired the way they moved, though they seemed so heavy and slow, they had the deadly elegance of thunder. One of them passed over the roof in which I was. The characteristic purple glow of their armor covered the ground with shadows for several seconds; and the sound of his energy as he flew, bounces in my mind even now. If I had been less determined to control everything, I could have noticed the eyes that were studying me.

Time passed and we found a big house that, despite being human, I loved. My father and I wanted to keep it, same as a group of Hunters who had also seen it. The leader of that squadron was one of the most powerful I had captured so far. I began to feel some liking for him, after knowing that it was him who had flown over my head, that day in the battle.

We agreed on the terms between the two small groups, hoping that our life in the new world would become like the one we had. Together we would rebuild the great mansion. However, before such an agreement, the situation became somewhat difficult...

"I don't think we're going to need them, ma'am," he said, removing from his body the armor, which diluted like a trail of ink, to the ground. The spear and the hull were lost through the ground, and the rest became something thin, which marked all the muscles of his body. That was a garment similar to the one that was worn the rest of us. "Much better." He smiled at me, feeling his body free from that burden.

We were in a piece of land away from the house. The sky was gray, like every day of that war, which already seemed so far away. The air rocked our blond hair, it entangled branches in the locks and mingled the smell that our energies gave off. The Big Hunter, with an entourage of other ten, stood up straight a few meters from me, hoping to see what my next move would be. I watched the horizon, waiting for my father to approach as, I wasn't sure I could handle that situation, if something bad happened between me and that Hunter. Somewhere inside me, I knew that the community relationships would never be like before the confinement.

"Perhaps you feel insecure like that..." Only he had taken off his armor. And the only thing that my comment caused, was that they put the spears at the ready. Perhaps that would soon become a fight to see who would keep the land. I wasn't going on a successful path. "Having spent so many days with it," I continued, trying to look friendly, "it will be hard for you not to wear it."

That relaxed the tense atmosphere that surrounded us. It seemed that the conflict could be averted. I didn't mind sharing with that little group, anything that could be found by my father and myself; it was probable that they did not mind either.

"I don't think so!" He assured, categorically. He seemed very cheerful. My father suddenly appeared beside us, as if he had always been there. "Do not take it off, if you do not wish." He let a laughter escape. "It seems I am the only one who would take it off," he added, pointing backwards. "I don't know how things are going to be, from now on, but I think we can get it to look like what we had."

A wave of nostalgia ran through me. And for a few brief moments (so brief that it might not even happen), I forgot why I felt like this.

"So, let us seal a pact." I removed the armor enough to leave the arm uncovered. "None of us will try to take this land from others, or anything it contains."

"None of us."

The twelve of us extended the arm and let our commitment be etched with invisible ink on our skin. It was an oath that involved the energy that made us who we were. An unbreakable oath.

I assumed that the same would be happening throughout the world: small pacts, between small groups. After taking control of our home, we could return to the normality of a quiet and long life... Very, very long.

We approached the big house, which had two large balconies and two towers that flanked the main doors, which seemed made of stone; all the windows were gigantic and made of gilded frames; its walls were of a soft orange color, which made a rare contrast with the grey sky. The gardens were covered with dead flowers, which would soon cease to be a problem. I was flushed in happiness. Soon we could simply observe how the world was slowly becoming what we remembered and doing whatever we did before the arrival of humans.

My father and I had to give a display of confidence to the group. Something not as meaningful as the energy pact, but something purely symbolic. I withdrew from my body most of the armor; I left my head, my shoulders and my hands uncovered.

"Why would a human build something so big?" Asked one of the Hunters, letting the spear and the hull also be lost on the ground.

Apparently, my display of confidence, had worked.

"So big and so embellished." I added. "Look at the flowers of the doors." Making both, a frame and a decoration, some small dark flowers carved in the thick stone zigzagged until they got lost in the darkest part of the threshold. "Maybe they had the technology to do this kind of thing and not to defend themselves."

"Anyway..." My father interrupted. He projected his power towards the door, opening it. "Let's enter. Now all of this is ours."

Only my father, the Hunter and I advance; the others surrounded the perimeter of the house, so as not to have problems with any other group. The mansion had many rooms, in which were jostled pots and broken dishes; they were all locked, so I had to open them using power. I wondered what had become of those humans, for there were no signs of fighting anywhere in the house, yet everything seemed to be prepared to withstand a battle: the armchairs were crowded on the stairs, so that it was more difficult to access the floor upstairs. «Or get out of there», I thought. I began to notice that some of the windows were covered by chunks of wood impregnated with a black substance, of a peculiar smell. On the ground, there were metal artifacts, they seemed to be able to cut meat, easily. My father activated one of the traps with his leg, causing a roar that resonated in the depths of the house. It was a great metal rod, from which many sharp protuberances emerged. I touched one of them with my finger and continued walking towards the stairs, imagining a human leg being severed by the artifact.

At that time, I didn't understand that need to protect yourself from those of your kind. What I didn't know was that I would soon understand it better than I could have imagined. We found a lot of hidden weapons. Someone had taken so much trouble to protect themselves; what was troubling me was not knowing whether they were looking to guard against us or other humans.

If there was someone hiding, they definitely knew we were downstairs. I went up-stairs making every step to sound with strength. I felt that a strong smell came from the next floor. I scratched one of the walls and the smell became more intense. I raised my hand to where I felt the smell, because I did not want to give such an easy death to the human being hid; but I aimed far, I wanted him to feel that his end was close. I wrecked the ceiling and jumped into the darkness. I threw another blow of energy into the last layer of wood that was separating us from the open sky, so that the light could enter and he would see me come. It seemed that it had been an eternity since the last time I felt the smell of blood; I already missed feeling the flesh between my fingers and seeing how the life of those beings faded in the depths of their stained eyes.

I heard planks creaking under my footsteps and several whining that, today, after so many years, continue to reproduce in my memory, as if it were a gentle cadence immovable. And in a way, that day the time stopped and nothing was again as before: the air currents changed direction, only revolving around us, in that room; the day became night; the moon and the stars sank into the sea; and the fish at the bottom of the ocean began to furrow the infinity of the universe; raindrops hit my face and left gray marks, which were lost in the darkness of my armor. When I saw them, ah... when I saw them, I knew I was not going to see a brighter light again, than the one that those eyes gave off. Two pairs of human eyes, who planted a rift in my soul and that of all of us.

Chapter 2

«The Eyes of a Murderer»

I went through the wide abyss where I could float. I did not allow the fear of the shadows to drown me. I had a fixed idea in my mind: that night I would come home. Such was my endeavor that the universe allowed me to devour the soul of one of those monsters. «Something helped me escape..., to return. My God, perhaps?» That thought gave me strength and when I came out and felt the air caressing my naked skin, the fury disappeared and little by little, I realized that it was my duty to conquer that land. I looked back and I thought my brothers would soon come... Soon we would all be together and those beasts would have left.

Fragment of Hecate's lost diary.

We... had not murdered humans like those. Right? That question struck my brain, as a gust of cold air shakes some bones that are breaking. I waited for my father, hoping that he would be able to finish that, but his face was distorted: Our whole world was crumbling.

"They are..." I tried to articulate. "They're human."

"But smaller." Added the Hunter.

That tiny garret was crammed with wooden sticks and broken things. Some blankets covered what appeared to be a vent, or a window, and the stench of those creatures was a mixture of terror and rubbish. The two children were curled up in a ball in the nest that they had formed with blankets and fabrics, trying to disappear, so that we do not see them. And all we saw was the light that gave off their dark eyes. There could be nothing in the universe purer than that gleam. We could have spent eternity watching them, but the children needed our attention. Confined in that tiny space, during who knew how long, they barely had muscle around the bone and of course they had spent days without eating. I approached them and saw no hatred, no wickedness; I saw nothing of what gave off the humans who had died in the Great War; there was only fragility and love. They were so small... Very small. They were dirty and weak. They got scared when they saw me up close. I cleared my throat and tried not to look threatening. Although I was sure they knew I was a killing machine. After all, how a human could not know already who we were. I stretched my arm to them and waited for any of them to hold my hand. I wanted them to feel good, not to be afraid and I also wanted to have as close as possible that light, which activated at the bottom of my mind, something I dismissed in an instant.

For a second I felt a certain repulsion at the idea of making such contact with them and I wanted to withdraw my hand. I also felt an impulse that led me to want to destroy them and put an end to that uncertainty that overwhelmed me. It would be a secret that the three of us would keep, a terrible secret that we would have to carry. Would we be able to take that with us?

I heard a sigh behind my back. They too were overwhelmed.

I repeated in my mind that I hated humans; that they had expelled us from our home and that they brought us almost to destruction. I repeated it as if it was an assortment of sheer madness, which ironically saved me from not falling into craze. When the smallest child grazed one of my fingers, a shiver swept through my body and I knew I could never hurt them.

"Father." I whispered, feeling still the energy that they gave off going through my fingertips. "I can't..."

He advanced, with poise. He leaned against the wall, leaving a few little footprints in the wood.

"I cannot..." He said, in a tremulous voice. "I can't..."

It seemed that we both weighed the idea of killing them right there and ending that suffering.

"They are so beautiful." My voice no longer seemed to belong to me. The part of me that was a warrior, hated me. "We won't let them hurt them."

Terrified, I remembered, suddenly, that there was someone else than my father and the children in the room; I turned slowly, hoping not to see a great armed assassin.

"And we won't" He seconded. He shook the dust on the armor, as if that were indeed necessary. "If we show that light to the community, they will be convinced of the same as we are."

"And the ones who don't see it? Those who would only hear the whisper of some human..." My father was restless. None of us wanted a war between our own.

"We'll have to give them time." I stated, approaching the vent. I pulled the blanket off with disgust and tried to make a window that was rather a hole. The light poured in and blinded the two children for a moment.

"They are so pure..."

The smallest, the one who had touched my hand, began to laugh. Maybe he understood that he wasn't going to be executed. I told myself, for years, that I had not killed anyone like him; but deep down, I knew I had done it. I knew I had enjoyed tearing off the heart of children like them —kids with infinitely less luck— as well as I did with older humans.

Humans...

...Children.

"They must come and see them."

I looked at the Hunter, that matter was consuming almost all of my energy. I pulled my hair behind my ear and rested my back against a broken piece of wood.

"Then let them come."

Let them come and kill us all.

"My boys and I", he started to say. I lifted an eyebrow to this way of referring to his squadron, "we will support this cause."

I thought I considered those words enough, and I just nodded. At that time, the three together, overwhelmed by the situation, we petrified trying not to be victims of what seemed to be a nervous breakdown, without even noticing what those children needed, who withered with the passing of the seconds.

"Let's trust..."

My father left the room, leaving us alone.

"He has called other members of the community." I did not know what to do in such an awkward moment. The children continued to curl up in a ball on the ground and the environment was quickly charged with energy. I had not been alone with any member of the community since... since we were imprisoned. "You should go, so your boys know we'll have company."

"They know that already" He crossed his arms over his chest and adopted the same carefree position that I had. "We can wait for them to come and get them. He suggested. The sound of the children's hearts came to my ears; I was not very accustomed, at that time, to have living things so close and their throbbing, they distracted me. "Perhaps we did not notice this light in other humans", was he never going to shut up? "Because the heat of battle blinded us."

He kept his gaze fixed upon me. He was hoping I would give him an answer.

"Yes" I took a glimpse of the children. "That's what happened."

My voice didn't sound convincing at all, but I did enough to keep away those memories from my mind. I stopped for a moment in the body of that Hunter, trying to calculate the energy that he could accumulate to protect the two children if the community did not accept them. I walked slowly to the nest of humans and took one in arms, the little one, who had touched my hand. I did not pay attention on the dirt on his face and how malnourished he was, for I believed that all humans would be like this. I pressed his head against my breast, so that he would sleep and I went to the threshold, on which rested who would have to help me save them. I was hoping he would understand that he had to take care of the other.

"My name is Aingeru." He said, all of a sudden. I turned around until I found his light blue eyes. He had just revealed his name. "In some places in this world, that word means..."

"... Angel." I stopped him. Inadvertently, I pressed the child too strongly against my body, that I caused him some bruising. "I cannot..."

I tried to tell him that I couldn't tell him mine —I wasn't even sure I could even pronounce it out loud— when he walked towards the other child, who didn't make it easy at all, and that put an end to our conversation. I was already on my way to the yard when I knew he had accepted it.

That Hunter had revealed to me his name, something that we all kept as our greatest treasure. I wondered what it was that led him to do it so, maybe it was because he wanted to show us that we could trust them or there might be something else.

I didn't know how to feed the human, but for the moment, I gave him some of my energy so he wouldn't die. I arranged one of the rooms of the great house: I pushed aside the dust and knocked over the wooden planks blocking the entrance of the light and the fresh air; the currents made the boy laugh out loud for several minutes. I liked to see him laugh: his round, clear eyes gave off a light that caressed my soul. When I finished, I stood beside him, on the bed, from which I had already made his second nest. I approached with apprehension the hand to his head, I wanted to touch his hair, but I withdrew it before even rubbing it. I really believed that, despite being human, our people would gladly accept him... if they approached that abyss and looked inside.

Many were the ones who refused to go; so many others, were deployed around the house, fearing that we would have gone mad; letting us be clear that if we lied, a new battle would resonate in the world. A large part of the community gathered that same day. I saw them in the sky forming a thick black spiral, which oscillated in the distance; their hiss came to the child's room. I stood still at the window, watching them all enter the great house. I saw my father and Aingeru, franking the door. «They will soon be here», I thought. And what seemed a shiver swept through the tips of all my pores. I didn't like that idea. Why wouldn't they trust in our word, without further ado?

I went down to the living room of the house when they were already all together. More members had come than I had ever seen in the same place. I felt some pressure in my stomach believing that I might have to face all of them if they decided that humans should die.

I was hardly able to look at their faces, for they all returned a tense expression that made me feel uncomfortable.

"Before we begin," said Aingeru, enclosing everyone with a broad hand gesture, "I would like to say what I felt when I saw those two children when we found them."

"How opportune!" Exclaimed a Hunter who came out among the great columns of that immense hall. "The exemplar Aingeru wants to join the king and save the only two humans that his daughter likes." He added, without looking at me.

An exclamation escaped from inside our mouths. He had pronounced his name... He had not only insulted a superior, but he had done it before us. That act was a great insult. To utter the name of one of us meant that there was a degree of complicity, love, and affection; humiliation or, as it had just happened, that could also leave a challenge in the air. The atmosphere was rarefied and the electricity filled our bodies instantly, as if we were prepared for a battle. One question arose in my mind: were we really going to fight among ourselves? Would we really behave like the creatures that we so hated?

In Aingeru's face, which was contracted by rage and confusion, the desire to strike against him was clearly reflected. I fixed my attention on the other one and his conceited expression made me sick. His eyes were ajar, outlined by a fine purple line, and the blond curls fell to his neck.

"What...?" Asked Aingeru to the daring Hunter. He walked towards him, with a restrained step. His blue eyes were wide opened, sparkling in anger. And I couldn't help but to remember the moment he told me his name.

"Haven't you heard me?" The irreverent Hunter had a soft, firm, very powerful voice. "Aingeru, a traitor, lover of humans..."

Aingeru pounced upon him with a roar. They went through the wall of the house, rolled over the asphalt of the entrance. The one of the gilded curls, got rid of his attacker without apparent exertion; he twisted his lips at the same time as he kicked Aingeru, who landed without difficulty a few meters away. I saw a flash of green energy erasing the area outside the room momentarily.

I took my hand to my head.

Inadvertently, we had become spectators of one of the first violent scenes of our second history. Our whole world was shaking. These two children would lead us to total destruction, if we did not manage to redirect that absurd situation. I didn't talk much and so the words got stuck in my mind, despite wanting to refrain them.

"Enough." I muttered. No one seemed to hear me.

I sighed. I supported my weight on one leg, waiting for the moment when they decided to put an end to the fight. I watched all the movements that were performing in front of us, believing again that perhaps someday I might need them in some combat... I pushed that thought out of my mind, as that could only make me more upset. I heard a crunch when Aingeru counteracted the other's tackle, turning the hip and striking on him two aerial kicks. His opponent fell back against the ground and got prepared for a new assault. That would never come to an end. I concentrated the energy in the palm of my hand and threw it against them, hurling them violently towards a nearby river.

"Enter the house." I ordered. "Look what you've done! You've wrecked everything."

I watched them walk reluctantly until they stood in front of the stairs. They had the same height and the same muscle tone, but blond hair marked their faces differently. I hoped, in vain, that both would try to stay in the background, but Aingeru hurried to speak again. I wondered if he would always be so impulsive.

"It is our duty", he said, with exaggerated hand movements, "to keep those children alive. We don't want to be like them," he put a hand on his chest; "we mustn't annihilate everything without taking notice of purity."

"You're contaminated", fired the other one. "They're human! Don't you realize? I can't believe you're thinking of letting them live." He added, looking at my father and me.

"We will not be beasts." He answered coldly to him and with an authority that surprised him.

For a second I saw his eyes were of a different color from ours. Now I wonder why it didn't seem strange at the time? What was inside him capable of make me obviate those details? What was there at the bottom of that mind?

"They are innocent creatures" said Aingeru. "They can stay here and improve with us."

The other one laughed, almost madly.

"And you pretend", he drew with his hands a circle in the air, that we tell them that we annihilate those of their kind, for having snatched the world from us?" He let his words to reach us all at the bottom of our consciousness. "Will we tell them that they are not like us, but that they should thank us?" He made a pause to look at my father. "Will we give explanations to some humans?" His voice acquired some degree of sarcasm. "Or will we kill them when they grow up and you don't like them anymore?"

My father closed his eyes, as if he needed to clarify his ideas; but I knew he was controlling his growing anger. We were still not able to understand that something was going wrong. How naïve we were to think that we only had to kill the humans to be happy! Going back to our beginnings was proving to be more difficult than we thought. And I was pretty sure I couldn't even put a finger on those times again. It was clear that our hatred had consumed us too much and any change would make us see things from a more radical point. It was true that thanks to having waited so long, our energy had increased at a stratospheric level and we could perform incredible feats more quickly than we once did. But to find those creatures... those children, had opened a gap in the heart of our nucleus. A gap that we had not yet perceived and was going to wait, latent and odious, to the worst of moments to explode.

"The children," my father said, "will live," he approached a hand to his chest, closing it in a fist. "If one day they change," he let his words floating in silence, "we will kill them."

"You will soon pay for this error," he added. I gave a look to the Hunter, who returned me a full of the deepest rage that someone has been able to dedicate to me. When I realized, he was already gone.

It took us several years to hear from the community again. We cleaned the big house and distributed ourselves in the rooms. All that thorny affair of the children seemed to have ended completely... it seemed. And at last, incredibly, the world was once again ours.

One day I saw them from the roof, I discovered myself enjoying the tender scene: they played with a ball throughout the whole garden, they stumbled on it, and they also rolled through the grass until they get their feet wet in the river. The sun drew glimpses of the slight waves that were created with their movements. I still hadn't regretted saving them. I looked again at the sky and saw that the moon would soon come again; the clouds began to darken and the sky acquired an orange tone that was engraved on my pupils. I was happy; I liked that place, that's why I didn't want anything to go wrong and so I was willing to distrust even my group.

I fell in front of the heavy entrance door. I looked back at the flowers that bordered the frame and I felt overwhelmed. I decided to walk, to remember what it was like to move all the muscles without the help of energy and thus, I could achieve to avert my mind from the fight, which still remained present in my memory. Surprisingly, even though the door weighed an awful lot, I liked being deactivated. I watched the interior of the great hall, it was all cleaner than the last time: the high ceilings and the great staircase were gilded and covered with jewels; someone had installed a chimney in the back of the room and the sofas were very red, so soft that I wanted to lose the rest of the day stroking them.

"Ah..." I sighed.

I thought I had not gone around the whole house, so I decided to take a walk to get to know it better. I went upstairs, feeling the weight on my knees. I got accustomed to walking and moving at the speed of a human; I laughed alone as I went through the halls and the rooms. They were decorated with great small details that, at that time, did not impress me. I got into a room that had not been reformed. I heard a little creaking at the bottom of the stay, so I decided to go in and check what was happening. I didn't think there was any danger inside our house, so I didn't even get activated. When I was in the middle of the stay, I realized that they were the beams of the house, which had already given way to my weight when I wanted to go back. The ground crumbled and I fell down with it; I thought that it would be the last time that I would deactivate. Annoyed, I got up quickly, shaking the dust that had stained my armor. And that's when I saw him. Those black eyes looked at me, framed with a supernatural blond hair that had grown even below his chin. Has it been that long since we first met? The little human was barely rising from the ground and had opened his eyes widely: he was terrified. I tried not to move, so as not to frighten him more than I should; I wanted him to leave, but I didn't want him to leave scared. I did not know what I could tell him to reassure him, for I had never seen myself in the need to deal with a human. I cursed the moment in which I wanted to turn off some of my energy to move my muscles; If it hadn't been for that, I would never have fallen.

I stopped to look at his eyes, they gave me back the image that I was giving. I felt that any human would be frightened to see me and more if it was a child. I didn't want him to be afraid anymore... I remember a flash when a sigh came out of his lips. Little by little he sat up until he stretched out with shame before me. And he gave me a flower; a rose. I looked at him with the greatest surprise that my face could express. A small stream of electricity pierced my fingers through the flower and I saw something I had not been able to see in our first encounter: I saw part of his soul. I felt trapped by his strange gesture. The truth is that I was captivated by those eyes, just like that rose did. Its fragrance swept me up and down and I felt that I was surrounded by hundreds of flowers with its fresh scent.

I watched the little human under the last rays of sunshine. His round face and his cheeks brought to my mind the distant echoes of the battle: the deaths, the shouts and the blood. Suddenly, another memory struck my mind: bubbles in the water and some long hair. I got transported immediately, I didn't want the human to see me like this. That was a memory that my conscience did not want to process; it was too overwhelming for me and soon, I didn't even know what I was trying to forget.

I buried my face in my hands, waiting for that anguish to cease soon.

"I'm never going to get rid of this." I said, aloud.

The armor warned me of the movement and I got up to stop one of Aingeru's arms, which had managed to get close to my back more than I would like to admit. The brief shock of our skins gave me a shiver. He smiled.

"There is a place," he said, pointing to the area where the sun had been hidden, "in which only flowers like that grow." He pointed to the human's rose, which was drying up in my fingers.

I pulled a lock of hair behind my ear.

"Do you want one?" I asked him, bringing mine to my nose.

The blond hair fell down his back, like a delicate waterfall and his smile was undoubtedly one of the warmest I've ever seen. His face was delicate and warm, he was always smiling, and it gave me peace. I noticed that he wasn't even wearing the armor, but instead, he was covered in human clothes.

"I think they will fear me less." I do not know how he had interpreted my gaze, as it almost seemed like an apology.

I wondered if all of us would start to act as humans, simply so that the children would not be afraid and never change what shone inside of them. I was afraid to see ourselves converted into human copies, just so they would never lose the light. How accurate was that thought!

It seemed that Aingeru knew what tormented my mind and stayed by my side until the moon bathed us squarely, telling me trivial stories about what he did with the children. I don't remember exactly what he said to make me laugh, I just know that that day, his eyes also captivated me and I let myself get lost in the immensity of those two clear skies. But when I stretched out my hand to set aside a lock of his hair, an image appeared in his pupils: a great yellow cloud, which broke with the blackness of the night. The wind from the explosion moved his clothes and several shouts came to my ears... One, in particular, was the one that made me react.

I didn't even think about it. I turned my back on Aingeru and ran to rescue the human child. I went through the path that was separating me from the main entrance but, as I went to the back garden, I saw something that, even today, makes me shudder: much of the ground was collapsing and it fell hopelessly to the bottom of a black abyss; as black as a monster's mouth. Despite not being able to recognize him at the time, it was the first time I was afraid.

"Run!" I shouted, exasperated at everyone's passivity. "We have to save them!"

There was a strange atmosphere coming out of the abyss. The soil was cracked in pieces that floated for a few seconds, and then precipitated to the bottom. I had to jump several, before I could get to the place where both children were. I held them too hard and prepared myself to go through the road to a safe area. Once I was up there, I took a moment to understand what was happening. I watched the big crater that had formed in our home and heard a roar that made me shudder.

"What...?" The question was jammed in my throat.

I felt the energy coming out of that emptiness. It didn't seem hostile, but he wasn't friendly either.

"Bruce," I heard a shrill voice on my back, "don't fall asleep!"

The human who had lost consciousness was that child who had given me the rose. I approached and sat him up him slightly. If I gave him some of my energy, he would recover in just an instant. The contact disgusted me in a way, but at the same time, it seemed to me as something magical. The warmth of his body helped me to remember that what we had done was right.

"Don't cry," I said, hiding his head in the hollow of my neck. "I'll never leave you."

"He is the true owner of the house," said Aingeru, gently descending near us. I don't know what could have caused something like that to appear. Perhaps..." he stopped himself. "Maybe it's our presence."

The distressed tone of his voice did not pass unnoticed to me. I looked up and found right in front of Bruce's brother's eyes. There was no light inside; there was nothing but hatred and resentment. They were two wells so deep that they absorbed us with the force of a black hole.

Chapter 3

«Making Contact»

Where's my world? Where's my home? Maybe I'm wrong and this is nothing but a terrible dream. I wish I could go through the stars and see again the land I remember.

Fragment of Hecate's lost diary.

And I left. I left the little human in the big house, with hardly any remorse. It was such despair that overwhelmed me that I could no more and blacked out in the air when I saw those black eyes that did nothing but torture me.

The decision to keep them alive had taken place because I was weak, unable to kill them before anyone saw them. Had it been so, at that time I would not have had the feeling of having betrayed my community for nothing. It was true that Bruce continued to keep that light in his soul but, if his brother had changed, how much time did he have left?

I had spent several days outside, enjoying the world, which received me as if it remembered what was the last time that I was there. Walking through the grass and seeing all the animals, I felt that I was in tune with all the creatures around me; and seeing all the immense space, made me smile and believe that really nothing was going to happen to us: we were not going to have internal problems, as humans had... even after one of them had lost the light.

I jumped from branch to branch, through the forest, trying to set aside all those thoughts of my mind. For an instant I thought I could run away forever from what I had done, until I saw him there. Aingeru awaited me, leaning on a log, with armor on and a threatening air. I approached him and looked him in the eyes, eyes that were diluted in my memory and I knew he was not there to attack me. We did not cross any word, we simply let ourselves get lost in the vastness of the forest and shared part of that great sorrow that oppressed us both. We shared heaven and earth with all the animals. We went through a stain of countless colors, which was like drinking directly from the energy of the world. I didn't want that feeling to ever end. However, nothing I saw made me forget what I was leaving behind...

One night I heard a howl in the distance, it seemed the call of a lone wolf, but then I heard another series of howls and I understood that it was a herd. They were not a pair of solitary beings, unlike us, it was a strong group. I dedicated my companion a meaningful look and I could see in his face that he was also thinking the same thing.

"We have to go back."

"Yes," I admitted. "We won't keep on running."

Right at the instant in which we were heading to the big house, a thought passed through my mind. How long had we been out? I did not get carried away by the anguish and I was prepared for the reception that awaited us. A gust of air moved my hair. The sun projected the shade of the trees against the great house's main entrance, and that abyss continued to roar. Everything seemed to be in place but, there was something that was undoubtedly different: the children's laughter was no longer heard anywhere.

"I waited eagerly for your return." Said my father's voice.

A shiver invaded Aingeru and me. I could say that, almost in unison, we both put the knee on the ground, asking forgiveness for our cowardice. My father snapped his tongue and allowed us to explain what had been the reason for our escape.

"We weren't strong enough," said Aingeru. Although I was sure the only weak one had been me, I appreciated his intervention.

I observed that the Hunters who patrolled the surroundings, had the spears at the ready, and their full armor. I searched for signs of battle everywhere, but I didn't find anything to help me understand what was going on. Soon they swirled around the house's entrances and I knew that the signs that I so earnestly sought would be shortly shown. We were back in time for the battle.

"Sir", one of the Hunters approached to us, "we will soon make contact."

My father nodded.

"It seems that they have already realized", he restricted himself to add. He flew up to lead the group.

"Realize?" I hastened to inquire from the ground.

"They come to take him", said Aingeru. "They're coming to kill them both."

"What?" I exclaimed horrified. I was going to add something else, but I didn't want to say aloud that I didn't even want them to take Bruce's brother. "Where are the children? Where are they?!" I repeated, seeing that everyone ignored me.

"You should better get ready." Aingeru had also decided to fight. "We can't allow them to do anything that we all repent."

And if those who repent are us, I thought. It seemed that everyone was willing to protect the child that had changed, if that prevented Bruce from doing so. It appeared in my mind the moment when he gave me the rose, as if the remembrance had been triggered by a spring. I no longer had that flower, since it had withered so many days ago but, the ghost curled into my fingers with strength.

My father came down to my side, his cloak waved for an instant and languished on his back when his feet touched ground. He looked me in the eye, looking for a display of complicity. I lightly nodded. I would defend those children in that battle, if that meant that Bruce would not lose the purity that had conquered me.

"There they come", I mumbled, with a pouting of disdain that twisted my mouth.

A black wave appeared on the horizon, which was tingling with yellow tones. Slowly, it was advancing with delay until it was a few meters ahead of us. They too were prepared for battle: their bull-shaped helmets flashed at the moment when a sunbeam struck their surface; the purple glow that they gave off, mingled with the energy of rage that radiated towards us. And in particular, one of them, irradiated it only against me. To demonstrate our obvious superiority, we adopted a carefree attitude and we left our heads free of armor. We were two flames burning in the middle of an almost desolated field.

My father lifted his right hand, giving them permission to get closer. The group of Hunters descended delicately within steps of both. Aingeru and his group remained in the air. The Hunter who had led the violent episode in the house's living room, came a step forward. His blond curls were hidden under the hull but, what he could not conceal in any way, was his fury. I did not begin to ask myself what it was about until it was too late, since I always assumed it was because I had rescued the human children.

"What does this mean?" I requested, without letting anyone speak before I did.

He took off his helmet and put it, holding it by one of the horns, with feigned delicacy, on the ground. The sun struck him in the back, which could make him look bigger than he really was. His face, free of all, made me feel a slight shiver but, it was so brief, that I thought

I imagined it. For a moment I also thought I saw that the color of his eyes was different.

"Do not feel offended, princess." He said, with a mocking tone that did not pass unnoticed to anyone. "It is our duty to prevent community members from being at risk." He looked around, counting how many he would have to face to enter. "It is I who should feel offended, actually!" He threw his head back, which caused his curls to dance. "After all, it was you who wanted to save them." He thrusted his gaze into mine. "It was you who condemned us all."

"How do you...?" I started to say but, suddenly, I felt the ghost of the rose between my fingers and I thought it would be best not to lose control so soon. "You can't talk to me like that." I restrained myself to add.

He outlined a conceited smile.

Aingeru's group went down until they surrounded us. We all knew we were about to lose control of the situation. I began to see the energy surrounding us as if it were barbed wire, we were preparing for a battle that would mark the beginning and end of an era in our history.

I turned my head and looked at the big house, I could see the two children, almost oblivious to everything that was happening. Bruce looked to where I was, it was something that started me.

"The children can wait", he went on to say, there is another matter that worries me more". His voice acquired a singing tone, he seemed to be having fun. "You have betrayed your race and you must be judged as such."

A skepticism exclamation rose with the wind until it was lost in infinity; maybe that was the last time the community cared about something that could happen to me. It all happened so fast; it was just a second. My father uttered a muffled cry and threw a lash of energy against the Hunter.

"Don't ever...!" He shouted, when his blow was already lost in the distance. "Don't ever address my daughter like that again." His quiet voice was just a sign of the great storm that stirred after his false calm. What those words meant for him was so big that, for the first time, I heard him challenge someone. "Bayron, don't you dare to address again to any of us."

Bayron, eh.

Despite wanting in the beginning to maintain a calm attitude, his accusation made me angry. My energy surrounded us both and a yellow lash made him fall to the ground. During those moments I was unable to reason, I just wanted to tear apart that insolent Hunter who, without getting intimidated by my attack, defended himself throwing at me a wave of energy. I saw its blue color before he even left it free and I jumped to get myself lose in the rising darkness of the sky. The air stroked my hands in the fall. I spun in the air, to return back to my position. I looked at him with superiority when his wave was lost to my back, between the foundations of the house.

He was furious. His face was distorted into a grimace which made him look more like a demon, than as one of ours. Bayron held the spear with both hands and raised it over his head, while removing the helmet away from a kick. I tightened the muscles, I wanted them to be ready to carry against a weapon of such caliber. A series of electric shocks turned my whole body into an iron mass that would collide with anyone... or against anything. I started the race in slow motion, I saw, through my field of vision, all the bugs that had fallen from the trees because of the wind, as if they did not even notice my existence. The Hunter stood up in the middle of the yard, ready to counteract my attack without even moving. He made a two-handed blow, which I dodged in advance, I turned on myself and stroke a kick in the center of his armor.

Suddenly, I heard a near shout; the only shout that was able to make me lose track of time and space. I lost control of the fight when I saw the two children so close; Bruce's brother was more ahead, almost ready to wade across the river, however, Bruce looked at us, terrified: he was worried about me. Somewhere deep inside of me, that made me very happy, though, that distraction granted the advantage of the battle to my opponent; who, without hesitate for an instant, made a thrust that hit me squarely in the womb. I would have wanted to dodge it, but he had lost a very valuable time staring at the humans. But I wasn't going to let him defeat me that way. I held tight to the Hunter's arm, which made his spear a handful of pieces that surrounded both our heads. Several of those fragments were entangled in my loose hair and I was given the opportunity to observe in detail his yellow eyes: in that being's energy was not shining any of our power and there was nothing inside of it other than hatred. He loaded his fist of energy to throw me away. It would not hurt me, but it would be enough to get rid of me for a few moments, so that I would not have time to inspect again what was inside. I did not know what I had seen in those two holes because, when they looked again, they were as clear as mine.

"They are escaping!" Shouted Bayron, filled of jubilation. "They escape because they know they must die."

We all ran in their direction and the truth was that I didn't know why they were running away, if we were going to protect them. I went through the edge of the forest, trying to reach them, before anyone else. There were several moments in which I saw nothing different than branches and animals. A thought flooded my mind with a scathing despair: we ran through the forest chasing humans, like the first time we came to the world... not the first one, the second.

"Bruce!" I started screaming, desperately. "Bruce, where are you?"

I saw him later, stumbling over a branch and hastening to hide behind a log. Another scene reproduced in my mind: it was me, scratching a tree; it was me, ripping a head off. I managed to get near him, more exalted than I wanted to have been.

"Are you all right?" I asked, too vehemently.

"I'm afraid." He stammered, throwing himself into my arms.

That gesture overwhelmed my heart but, as if it were two springs, my arms closed to his back, just as I had done that time, before I left. I was hoping he would forgive me for leaving him alone. I took him and I straightened up, suddenly a ball of energy struck me squarely on the back and we both fell heavily to the ground. I turned around and I saw Bayron approaching. Bruce was a crying ball, a few feet ahead. The first hole I saw in my armor closed too slowly and was provoked by one of our own.

"Brother!" I heard that someone screamed. "Let's get out of here!"

The other child had darker hair and an aura of humanity that lacerated my pupils just by looking at him; his trousers and boots had mud and water marks. I tried to get up to stop him, but another ball stopped my step.

"What are you doing? Can't you see they're leaving?"

"This time you will not be able to save them." His eyes lit up with such a supernatural glow that seemed sick to me.

I would only have time to save Bruce, who was closer to me and when he would see his brother dying, he would certainly hate us so much that that light which we were fighting for so much, would be lost forever, as if it never existed.

"No!" I yelped, though it was more a plea than an order.

Aingeru appeared, as if it were an angel, and before anyone knew what he was up to, he uttered a ray of light that hit Bruce's brother squarely.

"Ribek," whispered Bruce, "where are you?"

I had not been able other than to protect the child with my body, however, Aingeru had indeed thought of another solution: to sacrifice himself so that the light of his interior would not fade away. Now the whole community would judge him as a traitor, I saw in his eyes that he knew the consequences of his act.

"I knew one of you would betray us," Bayron's voice was like a blade. "Very soon you will do it," he added, looking at me with fixity.

He adopted a mocking pose before us and vanished into the air, after all, it was clear that none of us would flee.

"You chose to die..." I made Bruce sleep, all his weight fell on my arms. "We could have fought."

"I'm sorry," he restricted himself to say. He bowed on the ground, beside me. As close as he has never been before. "Do not disappear again," before I could know what he was up to, he surrounded me and Bruce in a hug. "If you leave, he'll be alone and I won't be able to bring you back. I'd rather save his light with my life, than to lose it in the war."

Devastated, I walked with the child in arms and Aingeru clearing the way. It did not seem that he was someone who knows how to be about to die because, the way he moved his body, he showed rather an air of triumph; and after all, that was a triumph for all, because Bruce kept the purity of his soul. Although his brother still lived in some place of the world, we might never hear from him again.

I gave the human to someone, I could not leave Aingeru alone at a time like that. Although I must admit that I was surprised to see him so docile and much more that, the sentence was to throw his body to the great abyss that Bayron had discovered behind the house.

"Did you intend to keep this..." he let his words floating in the air, "as a secret?"

That was certainly happening, the rarefied and sad atmosphere overwhelmed us all. Nothing I had ever dreamed of while being imprisoned was being fulfilled. We didn't have a better world, nor did we feel freer. It was all a nightmare that didn't seem to have end.

"I", said Bayron, proud of his victory, "I declare Aingeru, leader of all of us and former protector of these lands, guilty of high treason," he expressed, looking at me; he also wanted to condemn me. "I'll be the one who..."

"No," stated my father. "I'll execute the sentence."

He passed by my side, without looking at me. Maybe he thought I would try to insist on Aingeru's innocence and since there would be little to say, he wouldn't want to take a chance.

I looked at Bruce, sleeping placidly in another person's arms, oblivious to what was going on around him. For a second it passed through my mind that, if he were not alive, none of that would be happening. I drew those thoughts out of my mind, for I did not want Aingeru's decision to be tainted by my tribulations.

"It's impossible." I said. I felt my chest loaded, it was about to burst. I couldn't keep on talking for much longer. "It has been your fault!"

I looked at Bayron contemptuously before attempting to attack him.

"If you're going to intervene in this" he answered me, before I jumped, "sentence it" he took a quick look at us all. "You will not be able to plead him guilty", he accused my father, staring into his eyes. "You were willing to keep that human alive, just so that the other one was happy," he looked at me and I regretted not ripping his head off.

My power got staggered. I went through what happened in the woods mentally and there was no way to undo it. I put my fingers against my forehead, trying to reach a solution; if the four of us together sneaked out we could evade execution, even if it meant living fleeing from our own. When I looked up, Aingeru dedicated a look to me with which he told me that the decision was taken. He didn't want the community to be more divided.

Despite Bayron's undeniable triumph, I knew we were not finished. It was clear to me when I saw in his eyes the raging spark of vengeance. So many conflicts had created a vine that would grow rapidly around both of us.

My father was the one who officiated the ceremony. It should be one of us who took care of the execution and I could not carry it out, since he was stronger. It was a gray day, there was too much wind and I didn't have enough energy to look at front. My armor had frozen, as if suddenly it had no life. The Hunters of Aingeru's group, his closest brothers, created a corridor by which they would walk, while all the others flew over the place, several meters above my head.

I saw a figure in the shape of a bull, walking with heaviness to where I was. The purple, flickering glow, was fading at times. Soon he stood near me, just a few steps from the great leap; just a few moments from losing his life. I tried to glimpse a trace of his soul through the thick hull, but only the reflection of a lost gaze returned, it took me lot to assimilate that what I saw was not his gaze, but mine.

No other group in the community had wanted to attend such aggression. Each and every one of them decided to cut ties with us, saying that we had lost our wits; having took in two humans had turned us into savages and everything that was happening had been for us.

Aingeru fell to his knees right on the edge of the great abyss. My father and the Hunters who were bordering the abyss drew up to carry out the execution. I saw my father, suspended within a short distance from us, shaking his mouth; he was probably failing the conviction and the motives. But in my ears there was nothing more to be heard than the lament of a soul who could not shout; I never knew if the lament was mine, for not having done anything to prevent it, or that of Aingeru. The big hole no longer seemed friendly, now resembled a caged beast, waiting for its prey. The time came when my father had to go down to the ground. His power got elevated to the maximum and it tore Aingeru's power in half, who shouted. Now, without power, the hole would easily end with him. I crouched my head, as if that would prevent me from seeing how Aingeru was gently pushed to the bottom of the abyss.

In a late moment of weakness, I ran to the edge and stretched an arm, but it was too late. He had already been engulfed. I closed my fist with strength and frustration. Why had I not reacted before? What if I threw myself and looked for him at the bottom of those murky waters?

"It's done."

He forbade access to our lands to any outsider. We would never mix again. Now our community, wound to death, would stagger until it exploded into pieces. Everything that happened seemed like a cruel joke. I walked to my room quietly once Bayron's Hunters had gone. I saw what was left of us. Aingeru's brothers kept their heads towards the ground, but I knew their mind was lower. I was not the last one to leave the great viewpoint, as I had wanted at first and as I passed by each of them, I felt how the power that was beating inside us was going off. We all decided to shut down quietly any energy-exchange pathways.

Nothing would ever be equal to the first time. It was no longer clear to me that we would have defeated the humans. For, in my point view, it was they who were diminishing us. Even when they were all dead. Dejected as I was, I could only get to a room which was vaguely familiar to me and at the time of slipping on the warmth of the sheets, I felt some small arms surrounding me around my back. I had entered Bruce's room.

"Don't cry," he repeated, passing his hand over my hair. "I'll never leave you."

Chapter 4

«Assault Plans»

I observe them when they sleep, I see their beautiful and ungrateful innocence. Their eyes move frantically and it even escapes a word. They drown in what they call dreams. What do they see? Would they be reflections of their own existence? Will it be what they do not see, everything that torments them? I wonder what would happen to them if they saw what I see in a blink.

Fragment of Hecate's lost diary.

"Today is my birthday," his voice ripped the environment.

We were sitting on the biggest balcony of the house, away from each other by several meters and despite saying it in a slight whisper, I heard it as if he had shouted in my ear. Sometimes I thought Bruce was trying to test my abilities, to have a slight idea of how far I was able to go.

"What's a birthday? I asked him, more interested in the subject than I wanted to make him understand.

He lifted his eyebrows, as if I had an obligation to know everything. He used to make that gesture very often.

"It's the party for the day you were born," he explained to me. "We celebrate being alive for another year."

I put my eyes blank and rested my head on one knee. The cold air moved the branches of the tree just ahead, I heard a crunch and one fell to the ground.

"What nonsense!" I said, waiting for him to get angry. I balanced the leg I had hanging in the void and spoke again. "Do you count all the years you've been alive?"

"Of course!" He said, excited, approaching quickly. "That's what we do." I valued his intention to explain to me that strange custom. "I'm 15 years old," he informed me, smiling. "And you?"

I looked up to the sky, it was not yet dark and I did not see the stars. I tried to think about it, I really made an effort to figure out how old I was, but it was impossible. Why would I look at a detail as simple as the years, if I was never going to die? However, in order not to be unpleasant, I simply answered:

"As many as the universe has. My soul and my body are immortal."

Bruce laughed. He must have realized that this conversation would not lead us to calculate my age. I liked to hear him when he was happy. For his laughter balanced my energy. It made me forget what was all that happened on that land, which was already contaminated by the smell of death and the absence of energy. The only person I was talking to was him. After that terrible day, Bruce and I continued to see each other, in fact, I think we haven't been separated since then. He said we were friends. I did not understand that humanity's desire to name all feelings and all actions. I did not think it necessary to lock something as enormous as any feeling was, in a single word.

"Mmmm..." He started, but he stopped right away.

"What?" I inquired.

He seemed nervous, there was something he wanted to know, but he dared not ask. My curiosity covered all the bad feelings that crowded inside me. I made a gesture with my hand, so that he could release his question at once.

"Why do you all look so sad?"

I felt a snap in my throat and an avalanche of memories falling on me, like a sticky, suffocating mist. Why did he say that? Didn't he remember everything that happened that night? For a brief lapse of time I felt an immense fury against him, but, almost instantaneously, I understood that he was not to blame for my pain. He was not like the other humans to whom we had killed... The same people who had given it to us.

"We were weak," I responded, looking forward to talking again about how old we were. "And this world had changed us."

He understood that I didn't find pleasant to speak and he did not ask again.

"And what are you going to give me?" He sat down on the edge of the balcony with me, throwing his weight backwards. "Don't worry, I'm not going to fall."

I saw him stretch like a cat and I felt a faint envy at the contemplation of someone who lived in a world without worries. His carefree attitude made me feel better. And it occurred to me, all of a sudden, what my gift should be.

"If that happened," I stretched both legs, feeling that I was entering that world of him, "I'd take you before you got to the ground."

We kept talking for a few more hours, until he had to leave. I really wanted him never to lose that shine, because after those years I got used to the idea of having him by our side, as part of our life. But I knew that it would not last forever, either due to a change in his interior, or due to his natural death. How many years would he have left to enjoy them with us? The tiny compounds of his skin would soon begin to die; how much time would he had left? How long would it take him to leave us?

His ridiculous question about my age had been kept in my mind. And somehow it was funny to me the idea of counting, year after year, how long you were alive; or what you had left to die. I once asked him how he knew so many things about his species, if he had never seen anyone who could explain everything they did. He replied that in one of the rooms on the first floor, there was a big mountain of books and videos that never had an end. His enthusiasm for everything continued to seem to me incredible.

I stayed on the balcony for a long time. We always met there when he woke up. He appeared eating something and then he left; then I was left alone until it was dark and he was coming back, to make me more bearable the fact of feeling a tremendous emptiness in my energy. He said that I was like a gargoyle, some sculptures he had seen in the photograph of a cathedral, I stayed all day in the same position, on an empty and almost ruined balustrade. I should have taken some time to repair some of the places in the house, but I never considered that a reform would erase the memories that had been encrusted in that place.

I observed the viewpoint that we built after Aingeru's death: it should have been a set of precious scenes, to remember how great our lives were, before we got there; however, it was a symbol of death, which only brought to my mind, the echoes of a battle, a race through the forest and some disturbing eyes that, I was not even able to remember accurately.

I was very young when we were banished to... where? It was impossible for me to recall what had happened; it was even beginning to be hard to remember the prison. If only I had realized at that moment everything that was being erased from my mind, perhaps I could give the voice of alarm... I only kept in my mind slight brushstrokes of how spectacular everything was before humans. I dropped a sigh when I thought of them; how terrible they were. Why did they have that destructive urge? Why were they not able to see the beauty that was in the world and why they did not want to keep it? Why weren't they like us?

I felt an energy fluctuation when my father materialized near the door. I was turning back when he crossed the terrace threshold. He knew that I noticed his presence and I assumed that he would also know that I would not say anything; even more after he left me by myself for so long. It had been very hard for both of us to have had to execute Aingeru and to have allowed the community to almost get vanished, however, he must have had to be supported on me. He walked until he was at my side.

"I don't think he's dead."

That statement, no doubt, surprised me. I wondered if that was his way of telling me that he was already prepared to overcome the pain. For a few fleeting moments I thought we might soon be able to speak again and be again, at least, ourselves.

I still didn't see the stars in the sky.

"Sometimes I think he managed to survive," he continued speaking, worried about my silence.

I turned to face him, and what I saw at the bottom of his blue eyes, incredibly blue, was the reflection of mine. I felt that we were finally prepared to say that the time of mourning had already passed.

"Me too," I answered, I took his hands in mine and withdrew the protection of the gloves. "I too think he exists still."

That was the last time I spoke to my father.

The hours passed by and Bruce came back to tell me that he had got seeds to plant in the garden of the house. He always looked so busy and so excited about everything... He didn't use to ask too many questions and by the color of his energy, I knew that he trusted us, that he didn't fear us. He may even consider us as part of his family.

"Bruce," I interrupted him in his monologue. He looked at me in silence and waited. "Do you miss your brother?"

His countenance hardened for a few seconds. He sat on the floor, beside me, resting his back on the balustrade. I had my legs suspended in the void, I turned my head to get to look into his eyes. He had gotten wet noticeably, which frightened me. I turned the body to put my legs on the balcony and to get a little closer to him.

"I'm sorry," I whispered, frightened, thinking I should have looked for another time.

He, however, laughed. But it was a laugher without emotion. He wiped his eyes with his sweater sleeve and breathed deeply.

"It's just tears," he said, as if he was explaining it to me too. "I'm crying because I'm sad." He dropped his head on his knees. I raised my head and saw that the sky was black.

"You're sad because you think he's dead."

He raised his head quickly and surprised. He fixed his gaze in me, getting up little by little from the ground. I was still sitting and from that position he seemed bigger than he would ever be. He took me by both shoulders vehemently.

"My brother is not dead!"

His words and hands got me frozen for a few moments, but he knew that it was his pain talking, and his desire to believe that he had not lost a member of his family. I never expected Ribek to survive, but if Bruce thought he was still alive, I wasn't going to hurt his feelings.

"I have a present for you," I said, all of a sudden, also daring to press my hands against his shoulders.

"Really?" He asked me, excited. "You took the trouble!"

I saw his body in the moonlight. The idea that had been harassing me just a few hours ago came back to me. How long would I stay with him? He had long blond hair, it was almost as blond as mine, and black eyes like coal. His body was thin but I saw that his muscles gradually became bigger and stronger thanks to the exercise and his eagerness to try to resemble a human whom he had found in a photo.

"Come," I said, as I jumped to the balustrade. I had been a long time without running my energy and feeling that it was sprinting through my body from top to bottom, excited me. "Take my hand."

Without hesitation, he held it tightly between his and jumped at me. I placed him on my back and I transported with the moonlight to the place I had thought. Aingeru had been the first person to tell me about that place, when he saw the rose I was holding between my fingers. Now, so many years later, there were nothing more than remnants of dead plants. There was also a corridor crossing the meadow, bordered by a series of columns, although most were ruined, giving the place some warm and intimate atmosphere. We were close to the boundary of our territory, you could see the light blue layer that formed the barrier that surrounded us. It's one of the most welcoming places I remember. A good place to see how life passes by.

"I believed," said Bruce, "that one day I could take you in my arms."

I laughed. But I didn't make any remark. I didn't like to talk about his strength, nor anything that could frustrate him. Although in fact, there were times in which I didn't even consider Bruce a human. It was as if having spent so many years at our side; having shared so many things with us, somehow, he would have become one of us. But I always listened to his breathing and remembered that not, someday his heart would stop and he would die.

"Here's my gift, Bruce," I pointed with one arm towards the ground.

"I don't understand..." he said, a little disappointed.

"I'll show you," I announced. "Give me those seeds," when he gave them to me, I threw them strongly into the air. I looked at him, but he still hadn't understood what I was trying to do. "Watch."

Suddenly, the seeds began to sprout, exuberant. It was night and he was not going to be able to appreciate their colors but, he seemed astonished. He came up to touch one of the red flowers, he slipped and fell as long as he was on the cold ground. I approached him, who had begun to laugh very loudly. I sat by his side, in the midst of all those flowers. The earth had stained his clothes, and the little insects flew to try to feed on his blood. I extended my energy to cover him, I didn't want anything to steal even if it was a bit of what was beating inside him. I didn't know how much time more I would have with him, but I was going to do everything I could to keep him alive as long as possible.

"I love this place," he leaned his head on my lap. "Thank you. It's the best gift in the world."

"I like it too," I concluded, taking one of his tufts of hair between my fingers.

"You have never told me what your name is," he said, breaking the stillness of the moment. "Do you have a name?" He added, seeing that I did not answer.

I told myself that he didn't have to know anything; I told myself it wasn't a malicious question. I noticed that I had twitched my hand over his head and it would soon hurt him.

"I don't remember," I restrained myself to say.

I saw how disappointment filled his eyes. He was hoping that I would tell him who I was, but for the moment, he only wanted a word. He didn't want me to tell him where I came from, or anything like that. He just wanted a word. He was expecting that I wouldn't say I didn't remember. And it was true, at that moment, me knowing that nothing in my world was as I expected, who was I? I couldn't answer to that, not even to Bruce.

"Then I will give you one." He sat up as fast as he could and took my hands in his own, expecting a reproach, I suppose.

I thought that was the moment I didn't even know I was waiting for, so we would all be happy again. The world gave me another chance. His eyes that, though fearful, were cheerful, caressed my soul as if it were only a delicate feather.

"It will be a name just for you and me," I surprised myself saying that. That gesture was giving me back something I thought I lost.

Several tufts of his hair floated in the air. His smile completely covered his face and as a sigh he let free the name that he gave me:

"Angelyne."

That name caressed my ears just as the wind moves the leaves of the trees. I allowed myself to close my eyes and believe that I enjoyed my life only with what I had at that moment: those roses and Bruce.

"Like an angel!" I shouted and strongly shook Bruce's hands. "Thank you" I stroked his face with one hand. "It's the best gift in the world. Thank you, Bruce."

Thank you for saving me, I thought. We got up from the meadow and walked to the big house.

He wanted to spend next morning in the library. As I was in a better mood, I locked myself in there too. That room had shelves that came to the ceiling; several dark wooden tables and a large, highly decorated staircase that allowed access to a second floor; it also had huge windows, which allowed us to appreciate all the forest surrounding the house. But what I liked most about that place was no doubt that you could not get to see the abyss by which much of our essence had been lost.

"Can you give me that yellow book?"

I liked to help Bruce take the highest books, so that he wouldn't have to climb on those terrible stairs that would make him fall to the ground. That idea gave me the creeps.

"You wouldn't have to kill any dragon," I announced, after reading the title. "I would do it for you."

He took the book and set free a giggle, but he didn't answer me. He walked to sit at one of the tables farthest from the door, he turned his back on the window, as if he did not like the outside view and I wondered if somehow he remembered everything that had happened in those terrible days. I felt a chill for him.

I wandered through the library, waiting for seeing another day of Bruce's life going by. I wondered if the old house dwellers had been filling those shelves throughout their lives or if it had been someone else who had put them there. I saw an old volume that caught my attention, its covers were worn, which at first had been hard. It was noticeable that many people had opened it. I read what I could of the book's title, but I barely managed to distinguish one word: «Titans». I looked at Bruce, who was immersed in something else. I opened the book and when reading that they had been locked up by the gods in a prison from which they could never get out of, I felt a shiver going up and down my body. Maybe it was talking about us. I didn't know if it was best to hide the book or discuss it with someone. But that would mean disturbing the delicate atmosphere of familiarity that was weaving between us again. I left the book in its place, with a strange feeling of relief.

Maybe at some point in my future life I repent that decision, however, at that instant I felt the pressure on my chest was relaxing.

I approached the window to see the sunset. I watched the Hunters and my father enjoying the light that, little by little, was hiding behind the dense clouds of rain. The creatures that before Aingeru died seemed strong and fearsome, now only seemed fragile humans. Even my father seemed turned off, as if now they only cared to receive the rays of the sun. They reminded me of a diluted drawing when the drops began to hit the crystals. In spite of not having anymore the stone that gave them that aspect of ferocity that had captivated me, there was an instant in which I saw them as vital as before. I thought I imagined it, but I smiled.

"What are you laughing at?" Bruce asked me.

"I am not laughing," I contravened, putting my hands on my waist. "Just smiling."

"And why are you smiling?"

"Do you remember what was like the armor they wore before the...?" I stopped myself. Bruce walked to my side, at the window.

"No," he answered. "I don't remember any armor."

"Well, you would have loved it," I looked into his eyes, he was delighted. It was rare for me to talk about that sort of thing because, after so many years, it was the first time I expressed it aloud.

"What was it like? Like the one in the movies we have seen?"

I released a laughter when I remembered the cavalry scenes of the movies we saw when he was smaller, before he liked to read more. A set of pieces of metal, arranged by the whole body as a shell that, all it did was to tinkle and announce that you arrived.

"No, not like those," I kept quiet for an instant, trying to find the best words so he could imagine them as well as I remembered them. They were two pieces, formed by a material that was alive," I pointed out my armor, "like mine, but more resistant."

"Why was it more resistant?"

I shrugged my shoulders.

"They found it first, I suppose," I sat on the table and continued: "The first time I saw that armor, I felt that I was short of breath," I exaggerated, seeing that Bruce was more excited. "One of those Hunters lived with us," the words got crowded in my head and began to spurt out, "he helped me to come back to myself, when I lost track of everything," I felt the pressure on my chest. "He was the one who saved your brother," his eyes were widely opened. "And then they took everything from us: the armor, the union with the rest of the community and his life."

When I finished talking, nothing was heard but the rain. I felt liberated, as if I had gotten rid of a great stone. That story had been entrenched in my mind and if I hadn't taken it out soon, I don't know what would have happened. Bruce was pale. I didn't know if I had done well to tell him all that, but I couldn't back out, now. Sooner or later he would have to know, although surely now he'd like to go out and find his brother.

"There's a monster I remember," he muttered. He came a little closer to me. "I remember a monster," he repeated "on a very enlightened night. Sometimes I dream of that and of you," he added. "You saved me."

"I always will."

"And now that I know my brother is alive because of him," he suddenly became proud. He made a fist and turned to me, "we must recover the stone to honor his memory."

That idea was ridiculous. And I loved it.

"We will enter their cave as if we were two panthers," my story had altered him a lot, but I laughed. "And they won't even realize that we're there because we will be," he held a theatrical break, very close to one of the shelves, "two shadows at night."

He tried to do something like a jump from some human martial art, but it didn't come out as expected. He hit one of the shelves and the vibration caused one of the books to fall from up high, towards his head.

"Ugh." I said, looking away.

I approached him and got him up. He held his hand against the place where the book had hit him.

"You humans are very fragile."

"Can you cure me with magic?"

"Yes!" I claimed. "With magic."

From the first moment he had said that everything we did was magic. I was sure that he understood that what he called magic was part of our essence, but I liked it that he called it that way.

I exclaimed frightened to see that a red thread was running across his face, from head to lip. For an instant, he reminded me of all those predators who received me with a blood-stained mouth. But he wasn't a predator. He was weak and fragile and I had only seen the blood in a human when he was already dead. Worried, I removed the blood from his mouth with a finger; the red stain that it left on my gloves took a while to evaporate. I took off one of my gloves and tried to get that wound out too.

"Your skin is very hot," I got scared when I heard him talk.

I didn't even realize I was touching him.

"Or yours is very cold." I contradicted him.

I was glad to see him smile again. I looked deep in his eyes and to calm me down, the brightness that was kept inside, received me as always.

There was no trace of the wound on his skin anymore, but he seemed quite fatigued.

"If you give me a lot of energy, will I become something like you?"

I felt that an icy current went through my body.

"No!" I yelled. I shook his shoulders hard and went very close to his face. "Don't you ever want to change what you are."

He tried to run away, but I had a good hold on him. I took his head in my hands and with great care, I surrounded him with both arms. He felt overwhelmed, a little reluctant, perhaps, but he immediately returned my embrace.

"I am sorry. I didn't want you to get angry."

"I'm not angry!" I hastened to clarify. "It's just that... you're perfect just the way you are. You are brilliant!" I added, even if he didn't understand me.

From the first moment Bruce and I had shared energy, or magic, as he called it sometimes. Although I never thought he wanted to be something like me, I always took for granted that he was comfortable being what he was.

"So, what?" I asked, to break the silence. "You still want us to do it?"

"Of course!" He cried out, with renewed energies. As if that last episode hadn't happened.

But inside me the doubt had arisen. Would it cause any change in him all that we had shared already?

"We're going in the lion's den."

Now, remembering that trip, I feel the smell of my burnt flesh again.

Chapter 5

«Death Wound»

I cannot stop looking to the sky and contemplate the stars who laugh at me for having been trapped and not having the chance to return with them... will they be seeing me from the sky? Will they laugh at me for abandoning them?

Fragment of Hecate's lost diary.

No one was watching after Aingeru's death.

I was excited by the simple idea of being invincible, but the truth was that I liked more seeing Bruce so happy. He had never left our territory and that was like a refreshing bath after a long dry season. I wanted to ask him what he felt. But I couldn't find the right words so he could understand what I meant.

"Are you happy?" I said at the end.

We passed by a clear forest area, in which the trees were not too abundant, but they were large and pointy. The cold air stuck us squarely in the face and the stars shone high above the sky, like thousands of beacons guiding us.

"Very much so!" He cried out. "I'm flying!"

The little human was weightless; I was able to lift him with one hand. His blond hair fluttered in the wind and tiny drops of sweat were stuck on the ends.

I would never have believed that at some point in my life I would be holding a human on top of the black sky. For a moment I imagined that his fragile body would fall and would explode inside and in less than it lasts for me an instant, he would already be dead. That idea got me shivering. I didn't want Bruce to die soon. I felt how hard it was for his lungs to breathe and also how his heart was beating out of control, his vital functions would begin to wane soon, when the countdown of our human would begin to run. A moment that was not even in my hand to prevent.

We landed in a small river that we found in the forest and all those ideas were soon relegated to the bottom of my mind.

"This river is the one that goes through the big house." He informed me.

"And how do you know?"

He shrugged his shoulders and said it was on the maps. He was amazed by everything he saw and everything he touched. Feeling the fish through his feet and the night breeze, that brought the numerous echoes of the nearby animals, hidden to the eyes of any normal creature.

"All this is great," I gave him a hand to help him getting up. He was gotten wet a lot, "isn't it?"

He nodded and grabbed my hand tightly between his. His skin was so cold that, I could even notice it through the gloves of the armor. He glanced at the forest and his heart skipped a beat out of joy.

"It's all so...!" He answered, jumping out of joy.

Despite the work he had to employ in living, he seemed strong. I allowed myself to smile when I saw him running around in wet clothes. Although his existence was brief, it would be intense and perfect.

"Bruce!" I called him, when it had been a while. "You have to dry your clothes. If you don't, you might get sick."

His head was a yellow point among the bushes. I dried his trousers with the palm of my hand and we were able to continue on foot. We had to be more cautious from now on. Keeping quiet, not making noise with the feet —as Bruce did with the branches he stepped on—; were some of the precautions we were taking.

"And why don't you have magic gadgets?"

"What?"

I turned around him. He was startled and continued to speak.

"Yes, you know..." he hesitated. In my stories, the conquerors always have rare contraptions, which humans are unable to control or defeat.

It seems pretty logical, I said. I could not overlook the word that he had used to refer to us. «Conquerors». I looked at my hands, outlined against the starry sky and a bloody image made me go back. It was only for an instant, but I remembered all the deaths.

"We'll have to make a sword."

"Yes!" He stood beside me and opened his arms. "A sword this big."

We had walked for hours and the little human was tired. I took him in my arms so he would not wear down so soon, without even having found the whereabouts of Bayron's cave. I focused completely on what I remembered about his energy and I soon found them. They were so sure that no one would come near that they had not even bothered to hide. Anyway, who would try to sneak into their territory?

"We have arrived." I murmured, laughing. Although part of me was afraid.

I woke up Bruce to get in and began to wonder what a good idea it was to bring him with me. I felt slight fear in the smell of his skin. But if he was with me, nothing would happen to him, he shouldn't have been afraid.

"Uh..." I heard him say to my back. "Don't you give me any weapons?"

The only reason I didn't burst into laughter was because they would discover us. Bruce was a very funny human.

"There is no weapon in the world," I said, "that can protect you better than I can from those creatures.

He swallowed saliva and accepted that my words were true. His body was tense. Maybe he was thinking about how good that idea was also. I looked at my armor for an instant, it would soon acquire a different tone: the purple color. The moonlight was hidden by a dark storm cloud. It couldn't turn out easier. The Hunters were not even alert; if they didn't listen to any noise, they would never realize of our intrusion. I tried to find a weak point, but the truth is that they were well prepared, despite not having controlled over the entrances. We could not enter through the front door... or could we?

Bruce looked me in the eyes which were screaming what my intentions were. I heard a «No! », before taking him by the arm and running towards the door, all covered in dust. I threw a ball of energy against the big black hole that they had as an entrance, which also hit the guards that flanked it, throwing them away several meters. All the Hunters took several seconds to react, time we took in advantage to enter without any problem. I left Bruce on the floor, who was shaking. None of us could believe it was being that easy.

"That'll keep them busy for a while," I tried to encourage him a little, but his face only reflected panic. "It doesn't matter that you're afraid. Humans have it," I took his face in my hands, bringing it close to mine, "it's normal. I'll protect you."

He nodded too strongly. I thought it would be best if I took him back in my arms, but he wanted to walk. Quivering, he got up and stepped ahead of me. He turned his head slowly and asked me:

"Now what? Where are we going?"

That was my Bruce! We walked for a few minutes wrapped in a thick layer of stones. It was a big, enlightened tunnel. I was kind of disappointed about that den. I thought that we would find ourselves with great beasts and a cold black corridor; not with something so full of life. It was not difficult to find the energy that emanated from the mineral we were looking for, because it was so strong that even Bruce could feel it. Through the walls of that cave were dripping small drops that rushed to the ground forming bright puddles, the atmosphere was rarefying as we advanced. Bruce gave a slip, he tried to hold onto my arm but, after falling to the ground, besides the noise he had produced, he had gotten wet entirely.

"Gross!" He cried out, in a broken voice. "I hope it's not toxic."

I heard the Hunters stopped their frantic footsteps. They heard us. Thanks to Bruce, we had less time to find the ore and fade into the air. Luckily we were already close to our goal. It had a majestic glow, which still today, I could not see again in another material. Bruce waited for me leaning on the door's frame —rather, hiding away— as I walked quickly to grab it. Without taking off my gloves, I put a finger on its surface and tried to cut it with my energy, which hardly worked.

"How are you doing?" He asked me, with a certain tone of alarm.

"I've barely scratched it," I answered, distraught, by not having enough time and euphoric, because if with the energy I had used, it was barely a scratch what the ore suffered, I imagined what would happen to it when it would melt with my armor.

"Ange..." I heard him murmur. I completely ignored him, while I was trying to gather more energy, without reaching the overload. "Ange…" I overlooked his alarm tone and continued with what I was doing. "Angelyne!" He shouted at me after a few moments.

"What?" I requested, violently, as I turned towards him.

He was hidden behind a huge stone, next to the entrance, he only slightly took out the head, to observe the eddy of armed Hunters that were piled at the back of the corridor.

"Oh." I whispered.

I looked around, looking for some way of making time.

"We're going to get caught!"

I absorbed the energy that was separating us and I dragged him towards me. Bruce distracted me too much; it hasn't been a good idea to take him with me. Everything happened in slow motion, as if the seconds had become hours and every stride, an abyss. I had to avoid hand-to-hand combat at all costs.

But I had to take that rock with me.

I closed the chamber's door with a hand movement. I took the human by the waist, his beats hit my fingers, I thought I wouldn't hold that pressure.

"The last blow, Bruce," he looked at me, in horror. He leaned on my shoulders, trying to let go of my arm.

I concentrated a large amount of energy in the palm of the hand, an amount that I had not generated since the battle. It was a dangerous movement, because if it did not work, it would take us a few moments to escape. I couldn't defend Bruce from the Hunters if I hadn't got loaded, if I failed. And if we were caught before we had fled... we would have serious problems. It didn't seem to had been such a good idea, after all.

The energy spurted out of my interior, oozing all the pain I had kept by Aingeru's death. And also, the rage I had felt when the human traitor, Bruce's brother, had vanished into the air. The beam of blue light that was coming out of my hand soon became darker. It went through several shades and melted my glove, which dripped to my boots like a trail of human ink. Breaking that mineral was proving to be more difficult than I could have come to imagine, but I was certain about something, I was going to take it with me. When the light went off in the room, I checked that only about five seconds had gone by. We waited a long and distressing moment, until the great rock broke. The sound that it produced when it cracked was like a cry: a howl that arose from the bottom of the great cave. The stone was alive and I had cut a piece from it.

"Now we're leaving," I took the mineral strongly, which was throbbing with great radiance. "Bruce, get ready."

He tried to say something, but I didn't let him finish the sentence. It was all a succession of fleeting events: the Hunters burst into the great hall, carrying their spears at ready to run through us; Bruce turned his face in their direction and I prepared what I had left to take a big jump. I had too much weight with me and some of the rocks that we broke at our pace, while going through the mountain, scratched Bruce in the arms. That stone shone stronger as we ascended. As I broke the last layer of rock, I felt a great relief and like the triumph of a fulfilled desire it was expanding all over my interior. That impulse of new energy helped me to transport away from the place of the robbery. Bruce didn't seem so relieved, he was trying to let go of my arm, to run. I had to reprimand him several times. Didn't he see that if I let him go, he would crush on the ground?

"Come on, Angelyne!" He was screaming. "We have to escape."

"Don't be silly," I shouted. "Do you see anyone around here?"

He looked around, relaxed and fell heavy to the ground. He coughed repeatedly, he seemed very ill. I felt a huge disgust when he vomited.

"I never want to do this again," he laid on his side and breathed hard. "Don't look at me with that face," he groaned. "If you had felt what I had felt, you'd be vomiting, too."

"Don't be like that!" I said, approaching him and putting my arms akimbo, just as the human mothers did.

He laughed with my gesture.

"We haven't seen those movies for a long time," he closed his eyes and his breathing began to be deeper and slower. "Besides," he added, "after all, it was my idea."

We were in a clearing surrounded by trees. The river we had seen before, would be less than ten minutes away to the human step. There was a draught of air that I found delicious and fresh. I was going to enjoy that haven of peace, while my armor regenerated. I closed my eyes and saw with strength the colors that the nature gave off, the sounds of the animals that looked at us, hidden somewhere. Bruce had fallen asleep, he had been through many emotions.

"While you sleep," I whispered, even knowing that he could no longer hear me, "I will take care of you."

I couldn't believe that that ridiculous plan had work out. I took off the armor with some suspicion, after so many years feeling it against my skin, I was certainly uncomfortable not to wear it. The fresh dawn stroked my naked body and I felt the hair reaching down to my back. And I really felt very free.

"You don't know what to do with that, do you?"

I looked at Bruce with the anger painted on his face. Damned human, he had realized. It was no wonder, for I had been trying to melt the ore for over an hour. And I did not obtain any kind of result. When I touched the stone, it emitted a glow, but I threw my energy against it and I got absolutely nothing.

"We're going home," I informed him.

"Are you giving up?" He inquired, with strangeness.

"Of course not!" I growled, annoyed. "It's already dawn. We have to go back before they know we're gone." I laughed, when he was startled by a butterfly flying near him. "I'll hide it around here and I'll come back with my father."

I hid the rock at the bottom of the river. The water cancelled its energy and no one could detect it. My body had stuck to the armor as if it had been years since the last time, it was as if it was begging me not to take it away from me again.

"You left your hair down," Bruce said.

"Yes," I claimed. "In our territory I'm not in danger, I don't have to wear the helmet."

We went through the distance that separated us from the great mansion, at a dizzying speed. As we materialize on the edge of the forest, I felt something was wrong. Bruce was surprised at the burning touch of my hands when I stopped him and he understood that something bad was happening. There was no one outside the house, I did not listen to the revelry of the birds that Bruce had taken to my window and everything seemed very still. I stooped, dragging him with me.

"What's the matter?" He asked. The tone of his voice urged me to leave the place.

And suddenly, there was an explosion. The yellow flames surrounded the house, as if they were an incandescent crown, which also burned my pupils. I let go of Bruce's hand, to run, despite of having no idea what happened. The smoke coming out of the great mansion was dense and purple, the mark of the Hunters. That was an attack and it was probably my fault. Now that at last it seemed that things could go well, another misfortune hovered over us.

I heard Bruce screaming behind my back, I was hoping he wouldn't move from the site and that he would not put himself in danger. At that moment, I was only thinking of saving my family, but for a brief moment, I didn't know which direction to run for, because my father and the others could defend themselves without my help, but what about Bruce? That instant of hesitation, however, lasted little: Bayron got in my way, my father's shining red coat shone as he jumped, and it floated around him just in time to hide a gun that he pointed directly at me.

"You!"

I threw myself at him with a mixture of fury and fear. He smiled; I had fallen into his trap. I remember it as if it were part of a nightmare far away, far away... His face shrank into a satisfied grimace. As I ran towards him, he lifted the artifact and blew it up.

For an instant I thought it was a desperate attempt to stop the coup, but the moment the projectile hit my right thigh, I felt that my body was splitting. I've never heard myself scream. That feeling was something a creature like me should never experience. Now, I knew what the pain was. The coup had been so intense that it had burst my armor. I could only howl and try to take my hands to my leg, hoping to cure it, but my energy had vanished, it was as if I had no will to invoke the power that was beating inside me.

Bruce ran to me. I saw his blurred silhouette traverse swiftly the distance that separated us.

"No, Bruce!" I wanted to scream, but it was just a whisper. Couldn't he see I couldn't protect him from Bayron? "Damned," I dragged the weight of my body with both arms, trying to reach the human, "what have you done?"

"Do not get excited so soon," he dedicated a sardonic smile to me when I tried to get up. His eyes had a purple line much thicker than before and the blond curls were sticking to the nape. "We still have a lot left."

He put a foot on my breast and pushed me against the ground. That's when I realized Bruce's true trajectory. A black shadow next to Bayron. It was someone whom I thought was dead. Someone who had ruined my existence: Bruce's brother. That was the price for saving the light of a child: the end of our community; the end of all of us. And now, my family was in danger, was it really such a powerful plague? Oh, no. They are not, answered a voice inside me. They have won, because one of our own has helped them.

"Brother!" Cried out Ribek, swelling of joy.

"Go away, Bruce!" I yelled. After all, no one could protect him. "It's a trap!"

"You really care about him," said Bayron, bending over me. "You really want to save him!"

He took me violently by both shoulders and threw me against a column. With the fall I raised enough dust to see nothing for several moments. So much energy had killed all the delicate flowers of the meadow; as the cloud dissipated, I saw Bruce reaching his brother. I leaned on my elbows, trying to see what conditions the other members of the house were in. I crawled on the ground when I knew my best chance was to make Bayron angry.

"You would be nothing," I snapped at him, fuller of rage than of pain, "without that armor!"

He walked towards me, with a paused attitude. His silhouette erased Bruce from my vision. A part of me knew that we were not going to die at that moment, however, I was urged by the need to find my father and I wouldn't even get close if I did not transport myself. I tried to concentrate on the energy that was beating inside me, but I didn't hear anything. At that moment there was only pain.

"You and I," his footsteps made the ground vibrate. I felt like a badly wounded mouse who was listening how the hungry serpent approaches, "let's have fun," he stroked my cheek with some long, cold fingers, leaving an icy path.

"Stop!"

Bruce charged against Bayron, who got rid of him easily. He fastened the little human by the neck, who kicked on his armor, trying to escape. But the disadvantage was evident. I was going to witness another death. I was sure. Terrified, I couldn't even move. Energy didn't wake up inside me. I wouldn't be able to save him!

"Bayron, leave him on the ground!" Ribek's intervention surprised us all. But after all, he was still Bruce's brother. "Release him! I will not repeat it to you anymore," he threatened, holding between strong and firm fingers, another contraption like the one that Bayron had.

He shrugged his shoulders, as if he did not care at all what might happen to Bruce and to prove it, he let him fall to the ground without any further consideration. Coughing and red-faced by the effort, he crept to the place where I was.

"It's okay," I lied. "I'm not going to die from a broken leg."

"What about from a leg that doesn't regenerate?" There he was, another of his absurd questions.

There was a terrible pause. A silence that only wrapped us both. I knew that a battle was developing around us, but I was still not able to get up. What would become of us, now that we had been defeated? I wanted to enjoy a few more moments, before accepting completely that my community had been defeated by a traitor... and by a human.

"Brother," Ribek's grave and hoarse voice, broke the magic and the shouts of all who suffered the same thing as me, collided against my eardrums. "It's time to decide..."

I wouldn't have blamed Bruce for wanting to survive, or just for wanting to be with him. After all, he was the only family he had left.

"... if you die with her, or you join us," completed Bayron.

So, after all, I was going to die. It may have been a deserved punishment for someone like me; for a relentless murderer who stopped very soon being so.

Bruce got away from me, slowly. I felt that the cold environment paralyzed all the fibers of my being: my armor was giving up at times, dripping like a trail of ink, to the ground. A current of pain coming from my leg, paralyzed me for several seconds until, at last, I heard Bruce's footsteps walking away clumsily.

"This is what we were always prepared for" he told him, giving him his weapon. Bruce turned his head towards me, saying farewell, perhaps. "Accept your new destiny."

"Thank you, brother," surely, now they would ask him to kill me. I was ready to give up, I couldn't fight anymore. "I accept my new destiny."

However, what he did at that moment, surprises me even now. He took the contraption in his hands and triggered it against his brother, who lost his balance. Seeing Bruce, unprotected before Bayron, terrified me. I managed to exploit the energy that had been sealed inside me and threw it against Bayron, who lost balance for long enough. Despite having been little energy, for my body it had been as if it were an overflowing torrent.

"Let's go!"

I stood up and ran stumbling towards Bruce, he tried to hold on me and we fell, because I weighed too much for him. I got back on my feet, I told him to hold that gun tight, we would need it when we were hunted.

I glanced back, as I ran. None of them followed us, they only watched how we were lost in the thicket, they might know that we would not go far; or maybe they knew that, we would inevitably meet again.

Chapter 6

«New People, New Blood»

Now she's dead. And I've won. Soon everyone will know who I really am and my game would be over. If I can't go back to them, I'll turn this land into my sky.

Fragment of Hecate's lost diary.

What did all that mean? Had that been a hallucination? Would I have been intoxicated by touching the Hunters stone? We were trying to carry out a proper escaping pace, but in my own conditions, it was I who delayed the human. We ran through the forest, aimlessly, with the only desire to escape from what we had witnessed. The shadows of the trees now seemed to me great warriors who were chasing us and laughing at us. I felt in my back some iridescent eyes that burned me inside. I've never had to endure anything like this. I was in a state of total stupor. Having the memory of the shouts that came out of my lips; the vivid image of my community, suffering; the bearing of a human who had destroyed us all...

That image tormented me for years.

I fell again. I couldn't keep pace with the human. I had found that I was able to generate energy and project it, so if I got focused enough it could cure me and I could come back to help them all. However, the dangerous thing was that I did not control it. And I was too exhausted to continue, or even to think of trying anything; at the time, I just wanted to forget the pain.

"Lean on me!" He said to me, passing one of my arms behind his neck.

I got up. But as I expected, he was not able to bear my weight, his ribs creaked and I saw a wince in his face, which he tried to hide. We walked during what seemed like an eternity. I could hear his bones squeak and his heart trying to pump the blood to the whole body. I didn't see anything within two meters. He had his eyes closed, to carry me. He lost his balance and we fell, hopelessly, from the top of a slope. I saw his shoulder shattered when he got up, hysterical, to try to drag me, but my energy was depleted at times. I wanted him to flee; he could protect himself from them with the weapon he had stolen from his brother. But no, the human was hitting my shoulders so I would move. How was it possible that he had so much vitality and interest in only one thing? And it was at that moment that I understood. I was important to him. Just like my family was to me. And if I really wanted to show him that he was also a part of something in my world, I had to open my eyes and get up. I had to heal myself. With the greatest effort and waste of energy I had ever used, I managed to sit down and crawl to the trunk of one of the trees around us. Bruce seemed relieved.

"This will not end with me." I said and it seemed like a prayer.

I looked at my leg, which was still steaming. I felt a pang in my back when I moved it. I gasped when I tried to wake up the energy again.

"What are you going to do?" Bruce hesitated.

I'm going to rip off the burnt meat piece, I thought, but I didn't tell him. I wasn't quite sure what I was going to do. After all, it was an unprecedented situation.

"Oh, God!" He cried out, in horror. "I can't look!"

I laughed at his exaggeration. I was so stunned I wasn't even able to hear the sounds of the forest. My head was spinning and little by little I started to stop feeling the leg, it was as if I were losing it.

"It's rotting," it cost me more to say it, than to think about it. "I have to rip it fast."

Bruce had a livid countenance. I was hoping he wasn't going to vomit again. I was wondering if he would keep looking at me, or if he would faint as soon as I started taking off bits of my leg. The sight I had of a pale Bruce who was fainting, while I was trying to heal myself, made me smile in a way that seemed sinister. He staggered a few times, until he fell, seated on his rear. He was sweating. He was really nervous. I was no longer able to perceive his heartbeat and it began to be harder to me to distinguish correctly the environment around us. I had to hurry. I shouldn't postpone it more...

...It was now or never. I rested my fingers on the burnt surface of my skin. I felt it throbbing. At that moment a wave of aversion arose in me, for such was the horror that this situation generated in me. One, two, three, I counted. One, two, three; do it now, I would say to myself. And all of a sudden, I was able to block everything that was producing me fear, I was able to rip off one by one all the pieces of burnt flesh. Relieved, I opened my eyes and I checked, with dismay that I had not even moved.

A slight groan escaped from my lips. That situation was becoming more and more distant. How could I possibly be feeling pain? I looked at the human, but I was no longer able to distinguish it. Everything had become a thick layer of stains. I felt like I was falling backwards, hopelessly.

"Angelyne!"

I felt his cold hand over the wound. I tried to take him away from me.

"Move away!" I yelled at him.

"Let me help you." He insisted. I heard he was taking something out of one of his pockets.

Why did not I lose consciousness and woke up when everything had happened... as it happened to humans. The instant Bruce started removing burned skin from my leg, my mind went into shock and transported me away from there. Apparently, I still had a certain defense mechanism.

I went through the memories that were sweeter to me, those that already seemed unattainable old dreams. I saw my father's happy face and the soft, tender look of other blue eyes. I felt that I could get caught at that moment that my mind gave me and as incredible as that I seemed days later, I was willing to lose consciousness in the real world for just a few seconds to his side... In the midst of my delirium, I could never get to rub his hand with long fingers; I saw his face getting gloomy as I walked away, caught by a force that called me without regard. I listened to my name as if it were a distant echo and soon I gave in and I got carried away by that force. The last thing I saw of my reverie, was his face wrapped in shadows, surrounded by a long mane of blond hair.

A lash of cold air struck my face. All of a sudden, I saw myself leaning over that rugged tree. My leg was bandaged with part of Bruce's shirt, which was digging through the roots, to find food, I guess. I felt some pity when I saw that he had torn his clothes only to close my wound.

I moved my arms, to check the state in which my body was. Everything seemed in order, except for the heaviness that numbed my head. I tried to generate energy inside myself. I felt it was throbbing for several seconds. Expectant, I waited, with the misfortune of seeing how it went off without a trace. Weak, I raised my head and at least I knew I felt all the animals around me. But apparently, they were not interested in approaching me.

I sighed.

I tried to get up, leaning on the tree trunk, until Bruce's worried voice stopped me. He insisted on helping me because he said I was very weak. In fact, a crunch on my back proved him right.

"I don't think you have lost your powers." The way he uttered that word gave me a shiver.

"Me neither," I answered him. "But look at all the animals..."

"What's the matter with them?" He inquired, raising his eyes to the blue sky. The birds were eddying at the top of the trees, to observe us with thoughtful and almost menacing eyes. "Oh," he concluded, without further ado, as soon as he perceived it.

"Let's go!" I urged him. I didn't want all these animals to check the resistance of my bruised energy, nor would they peck Bruce's body to death.

We walked for several whole days, until the human flaked out and fell asleep. My body had recovered in that lapse of time, and almost no one saw the wound in my leg and the armor had begun to regenerate. I was still unable to create energy, so I always lived with the fear of an attack. I knew that, from one moment to another, we would be hunted. I looked at the wounded part of my leg, sad. I just wanted that enough energy would explode again in my interior to be able to transport us away from the threat.

"Do you think we can run away forever?" He asked me.

We had decided to spend the night at the bottom of a small abandoned burrow. I didn't answer. I was really frustrated not to have been able to heat the fire or to hunt anything.

I grazed the edges of my wound, which had acquired a strong red color, to prove that I still could not raise my energy. Weak, I fell on my back. It was getting dark and a light orange color began to surround us inside the cave. Soon we would be but a strong point of light in the dark.

"You should turn that off soon," I commanded him, pointing with my head at the fire.

"Yes."

He threw dirt over it, making us plunge in the dark.

Bruce had been asleep for several hours when I heard a few steps. It was a gentle cadence which startled me. I got up slowly and crawled towards the entrance. It was a dark night and the moonlight did not help me to distinguish between the shadows. I tried to use my energy to see whoever was walking in the woods, but I only got a crack in my chest. With a grunt I stooped at the entrance and waited. I pricked up my ears, and I knew there were three humans. They were getting closer.

Bruce stood beside me. I was scared. I recognized that in the shortness of his breath and in the way he had clenched his left hand. He wanted to take out the gun. Shooting those humans would be a fatal mistake, as not only that would tell them which our position was, but we would lose a bullet that would stop the Hunters when they would capture us.

"Bruce," I whispered. "Bruce" I said again, when he didn't answer me.

He had his gaze lost at some point at the bottom of the gloom. The hot air stirred the treetops and brought us a roar and a strong smell of gunpowder. The humans laughed quietly and tried to ignite a bonfire, like the one that Bruce had turned off. Apparently they weren't a threat to us.

I leaned back against the edge of the entrance, relaxed. I stretched the wounded leg which, due to the exertion of the position, had gotten numb. I sighed, relieved. That night we would not have to use our strength and we could recover from the big blow, I thought; until I saw Bruce's face in shades. Apparently he didn't think the same thing I did.

"I have to go down." He said. And his voice sounded like a statement.

"You can't say it seriously," I felt a cold hand against the leg and I knew there was nothing I could do to stop him. "They'll kill you just to see you."

"They won't see me." He affirmed.

He jumped out of the cave and landed clumsily on a rock, though seeing how I had done it, it almost seemed to be a feat.

"Why do you want to attack them?" The urgency I felt in my voice, made me feel really overwhelmed. And even then I could not guess what was waiting for me.

"They have food," he answered, as if it were the most obvious answer in the world. I tried to look him in the eyes, but his face was oriented in another direction. He began descending, without me being able to avoid it, but at the last moment he said, "We need more than that weapon to survive."

The strength of his affirmation struck me as if it were a stone. I waited, helpless, as he descended down the hillside. What would he think to do with those humans?, I wondered. Perhaps he would approach them as I did on the first day of our return; he might even wait for them to fall asleep. I did not care that a group of humans died but suddenly I got terrified by the idea of a possible change within him. And I really didn't want to lose my human.

I descended the hillside as I could. The leg was really a nuisance, which not only slowed me down, but forced me to make too much noise. I came near the human. He greeted me with a smile, overshadowed by the lights of the bonfire, which opened way towards us.

"You can't go," I whispered to him, insistent.

"Neither can you," he told me. Exasperated at my insistence, he took his hands to his head. "Okay," he agreed. He shook his head in frustration and his blond hair danced around his face. "I'll just steal what I can."

I released a little ironic laughter and a thought broke through in my mind: "He will not change".

We waited for several hours for them to finish drinking and eating. They seemed very quiet; as if the fact of losing their whole world did not affect them. Such an attitude told me that there was no one nearby who could help us.

Bruce came stealthily to the humans, who had been lying near the bonfire. There was nothing I wanted to do but run away. I had the heart in my fist and seeing the human wandering near them, I felt it burst.

"They're asleep," he told me.

"Something more than asleep," I contravened.

"I think this is alcohol," he said taking a bottle from the ground. "They use it to laugh and hang out."

"I don't understand," I approached him, limping.

"They drink until they lose their sense," he kept explaining, stealing things and keeping them in the backpack, which he had also stolen. "They use it to be happy," he added in a lower tone.

I looked at him in his industrious task, trying to find out what was really inside him and wondering why he didn't feel bad to be stealing from his own kind. I saw him crouching, running from one side to the other near those humans, and the desire to destroy them was not in me. Perhaps something would have happened to all of us; maybe I was tired of killing and that he would have grown so close to death that he saw it as something normal. He smiled at my eyes, holding between his fingers the shirt of one of the three humans. That was the moment when I realized that death didn't mean the same thing to both of us. And anyway, who was I to judge the way that human had to see the things?

I smiled back from the other side.

We stayed a few hours in the human camp, recounting the provisions and observing the maps they were carrying. We agreed to leave them one of the knives so they wouldn't be completely unprotected. But the truth was that we did it to prevent us from feeling that they would die for our entire guilt.

"Here," he handed me a wooden bar. "To lean on it."

"It's not going to hold my weight!" I snapped at him. "I don't want to walk with a stick."

I tried to throw it in his head, but he dodged it. I was losing all my abilities.

"Stop grumbling and try it," he urged me.

I tried to get up, as if there was no wound in my leg, but the lash that crossed my spine, showed me that indeed, that was still there. I looked at him with boredom and I took the cane with my left hand. I sighed. I knew that would break at my first step, but I wanted the human say that I was right. I looked at him with triumph burning in my gaze, but on that occasion the human would not give it to me; for the brightness I saw lightning half of his face made me shudder. A part of me really believed that they would never come to find us. But that light was unique in the world. Unmistakable.

I looked at Bruce, terrified. "What do we do", he asked me. I stumbled when I got close to him and I got to lean on something that I shouldn't break. I had to force myself to control my weight. Totally frustrated, I heard Bruce screaming when his body yielded.

His head struck with violence against the ground, causing him to lose consciousness. I cursed aloud. I turned the face to see how far had come the light that would lead us to the most terrible of deaths and I discovered that humans were no longer asleep. They had got up and hoisted metal rods, with an improper dexterity of that race.

"Bruce!" I shouted, shaking him with strength, "Bruce!"

I felt a cold hand around my leg. Startlingly, I threw a blind blow, which struck against bones that endured.

"Let's go!" Urged me a voice. "If you don't move, they'll catch us!"

Fear was introduced into each of the fibers of my being. Having seen the humans rise up against the Hunters, as if they were equal, had clouded my reason; I was so confused that the only impulse I received from the bottom of my mind was to rip off that human's head. However, seeing Bruce bleed, froze any homicidal intent I could have.

During that instant everything stopped all around me. I think I would have even been able to work with those humans in a good way if they promised to keep Bruce safe; but the circumstances led me, abruptly, to draw conclusions that were not entirely true. I wish I had not seen my human being dragged into a hole, as if it were an inert sack...

The other human yelled at me again. And at that moment I was unable to control what I had already stopped, just a few seconds ago. I threw myself upon him as strongly as it allowed my wounded leg; no member of the sub-race was going to address me, after having kidnapped Bruce. The human writhed vehemently under my attack. Surprised, I stretched my hands to his face and with all the strength I could generate I crushed his eyes with my fingers, but it was not enough. When, suddenly, a terrifying image was formed before me: a great hunter hit a tree, which caused thousands of splinters to disperse in the air.

That mistake helped my opponent to get detached from me and he placed himself behind my back, trying to immobilize me. A flare roared hard at his back. His silhouette was deformed, becoming a simple blur. The fire had harmed my eyes; my body was deteriorating at an accelerated rate.

Overwhelmed by the situation in which we had been involved, I felt that all the energy was extinguished, I was only able to remember everything that I had been through in just a sigh.

"What's the matter?" The human was screaming.

He pushed me against the ground and my body did not resist. The blurry spot urged me to get up and run.

"More will come!" He howled. "What's going on? Don't you see them?"

And no, I didn't see them. I was only able to feel that the trees exploded and that the energy that seemed to fade, had hidden somewhere inside of me, to protect the little that was left of myself. What was going on? After that shot, everyone I knew was rotting the same way my leg did. Who were those humans? Why did the Hunters fall with their intervention? They were just humans...

They pulled me and managed to introduce me to a very dark place. My eyes were closed because of the pain that had caused me the exposure to the explosion. I was surprised that they were able to orient themselves in that gloom; but I would still have a clear advantage in front of them, despite not having my energy nor my body at full performance and it was that I did not see through the eyes, I saw with the soul.

"Her leg is broken." Said one of them. "She can't walk."

They had been left on the floor, with much more care than I would like to admit. Apparently, we were in a long, humid tunnel. Two stout humans carried Bruce in their arms; I was relieved to see that he was well.

"... We almost couldn't even drag her over here."

"There is a reason why she weighs so much," another intervened. I deduced that it was the same person with whom I had struggled.

A heavy silence arose between all humans and I could soon feel their hearts pumping their blood without control. I knew what everyone thought at that very moment. I had remained with my eyes closed throughout their conversation. But at that instant, I saw my chance to frighten them; I couldn't run away, but I would dissuade them from touching me.

I opened my eyes and they screamed.

I felt satisfied for the first time in the day. The humans, terrified and with their backs attached to the wall, did not know what their next move should be.

"We have to leave," said one. He was tall and had brown hair, he was holding one of those metal rods in his right hand.

"But what do we do with her?" inquired the man closest to him. "She is one of them," his voice was transformed into a sigh when he uttered *them*.

"For God's sake, Francis," the tall human high seemed to be the leader of the group. I saw a scar on his cheek, which ran through half his face. "She didn't even attack us. And she was along with this kid."

"So, what do we do?" Replied Francis. "Bob!" He shouted again, when he was turning around to continue walking.

"We're going to take her with Hecate," he said, looking at me, as if it should matter to anyone who they wanted to take me to. "She'll know what to do with both."

Chapter 7

«Fresh Blood»

They have been long the years that we have survived to all the massacres of humanity. It's been hard keeping my loyal followers hidden, my family. What should I do now that I'm dying? Dying...

Fragment of Hecate's lost diary.

The humans dragged us through an endless corridor where, at least, there was only darkness. Maybe I just had to rest to fully recover the potential of my energy, but I couldn't afford to go after them; I didn't know if the hatred I felt would start beating inside me, if I saw them all again. Although Bruce was taken a few steps behind me, I did not want to be at the end of the march. I was in second position, while the human Bob walked with a firm and determined step, the only one who seemed not to be worried about my presence. Francis, on the other hand, was terrified; I tightened the neck's muscles to direct him a look of boredom.

"Oh, God!" He shouted, hysterical. "She's going to kill us all!"

A faint murmur surrounded us all. I felt that I would soon have to do more than drag my leg over the floor. Damn human, in the end I was going to really regret not having the chance of ripping his eyes out.

"That's enough," Bob intervened, reassuring everyone else.

Humans did not seem to be so frightened when he spoke; it was when Francis opened his mouth when the atmosphere got rarefied. They had even suggested taking me in their arms, of course between all and sundry, for they could not have had my weight; they even seemed nice. They had something I liked; and also, something that I was starting to get fed up with.

"If she has not wanted that you carry her," Francis stammered, "it is because she wants to have us all at hers mercy..."

"Human," I said out loud. The silence that collapsed upon us moved the specks of dust that floated round our surroundings. "If I listen to you again, I'll rip your head off with my remaining leg."

For a long while everything continued calm. A disturbing calm, for I did not know how the others would react. The human Francis began to tremble. His gaze was lost, as if his mind had been stuck in some already buried memory. He stammered unintelligible things, when he took his hands to his crotch and crouched his head.

"Did you pee yourself?" Inquired one of those who carried Bruce, who was quiet despite the situation. "Puff," he continued. "A being of the depths" «depths» "has had to tell you, but it's about time somebody did it."

Bruce stirred in an uneasy sleep. He had endured a strenuous journey and a great burden upon his shoulders. I hoped that having faced his brother would not torment him in any way. He was filthy, bruised, and his clothes tattered; although for me he was still shining, even after I lost most of my life energy, I kept seeing that light that conquered us all.

We continued to walk through the endless tunnel. The leg was really a nuisance. I was trying to move at an acceptable speed, even if it meant feeling waves of electricity passing through my back. Nor did I want humans to see that I was weak and fragile. So, I tried to walk by dragging it as little as possible, trying not to look as if I were pretending to be strong.

"Hang on," Bob startle me, turning around. He leaned on the floor over his backpack and extracted a little round contraption from it. "They don't seem to follow us... But we must hide the trail."

I didn't understand why he was addressing me. As if I cared what they were going to do! The humans curled up in a ball, they covered Bruce between two of them and Bob, their captain, pressed the only button of the contraption. Then I felt a roar bursting at the beginning of the tunnel. I saw as a great light ascended to our position, with a ruthless ferocity. The wave came first, which pierced my body without me even noticing it, I was glad to see that my flesh did not peel off so easily from the bones. I stood up until the humans felt in the condition to resume the march. Their ears ached and their clothes were lightly scorched. It was gratifying to see that I was still stronger than them. I was hoping all the energy would flood me again.

"We've been watching this land for months," he explained to me, it was all so strange. "This party was too trusting," how could he talk about trust when he was telling me that? "When you appeared, we thought we would have to abort the plan. And look at you!" He laughed out loud. "We were thinking that we saved two poor kids, when in fact we were rescuing one of them and her..." He looked at me, waiting for me to give a name to Bruce.

"He's my friend," I said, feeling that my throat was pierced, because he was so much more than a friend, he was something I couldn't lock up in a word.

I had responded to one of those creatures. However, he does not seem to me a human like all those whom I had killed in the dispute for our world. I watched him walk before me and I watched him as if it were the first time I saw one; like when I found Bruce and his brother. Was it possible that there were more, apart from them two? And it was then when I remembered a detail that had overlooked. «We will take them with Hecate», said the human. And the admiration that had risen in their faces when they thought about the possibility of seeing the person they were talking about again, lit up their faces and gave them the courage to face that situation.

We began to approach the end of the tunnel, I saw a white light that made me squint my eyes. But I had already understood how those poor humans had been able to defeat the Hunters.

"Human," I called him, with a calm tone of voice. He turned, also slowly. I leaned against the wall. "I know why you're not scared", his countenance darkened and my voice seemed only a floss. "Who are you taking us to?"

"We have little time before all of this falls apart," was the only thing he said. "I was not in a position to reply, I felt a cold sweat numbing my head. "Let's go!" he urged me, stretching his hand towards me.

Disgusted and very suspicious, I took my hand to my leg. It was cold, but I could keep on leaning on it. The human understood and did not add anything. Suddenly, a scream caught our attention.

"Where am I?" That was Bruce's terrified voice. "Let me go!"

I jumped and fell on the ground. I was scared. He had not seen anything after the Hunters' light, and he surely believed that we had been made prisoners. He had not even realized that they were human.

"Bruce! I called him, trying to get to him. "Bruce, take it easy!"

"Where...?" His voice was scarcely a sharp whisper, which was lost in the depth of the tunnel.

I tried to get close to him, but my leg failed and I fell to the ground. I had little time left. Very little. I was really scared. Would I eventually die surrounded by humans? Would I leave Bruce alone and lost in a world he wasn't prepared for?

"What are we doing here?" He inquired, hiding the trembling of his voice. "Who are all these people?"

Bruce pulled me to try to get up.

"Little one, you'll have to leave all those questions for later," Bob intervened. "The girl has little time left and we still have to transport ourselves."

That did completely disorientated me.

"What?" I required. "Transport?"

If any of them were able to get us out of there, using their energy, it was clear that a creature like me had given them that power. That would explain how a simple group of humans had defeated some Hunters, as careless as they were. But how powerful was the creature we were going to meet, if she had lent so much energy to seven humans? Maybe it was that energy that made me notice them as different beings.

"We've blown the tunnel," explained another of the humans. "It'll take a little while to come down. We have to transport to our base. There, Hecate will help you!"

"Who's Hecate?" Bruce was exasperated.

"I don't know," I confessed to him. "I think it's someone like me," his eyes got wide opened.

"Then we're in danger."

Such a statement caused the humans to release an exclamation.

"You have nothing to fear," Bob stooped by our side, "she's not going to hurt you."

«She».

Bruce shook his head. He seemed very nervous; I could not hear his heart beating, but the tone of his words was too hasty to be someone in a state of ease.

"Don't you understand?" He cried out, with tears in his eyes. "If we get near any of them, my brother will find us and kill us."

Suddenly and like a mace, the memories of that day came back to my mind. What would become of them without me? What would become of me without them? Nostalgia gave me energy to go ahead and risk taking the last chance we were given.

"No," I said, emphatically. "Bayron and he have stayed at my house; in my land," I grabbed strongly to a rock that protruded from the wall. "He won't come for us. He can't suspect we found someone we didn't even know."

"You don't understand," insolent human! "He wants to rule over everyone. Why else would he attack first the strongest of the groups?"

I didn't want to hear him. But he really seemed to make sense.

"Do you speak of an attack among yourselves?" Bob was trying to hide his surprise. "That's not possible. You are..."

"Apparently", I said, "we are nothing anymore." I tried not to make the pain in my body visible.

Recognizing that the sub-race had led us to destruction was a bitter pill. I used all the strength that gave me that thought to make a titanic effort, to allow me to stand up again. Bruce hurried by my side so I could lean on him.

"This time I will not fall on you," I promised.

He laughed tremulously.

We walked quietly during the brief journey to the end of the tunnel. The humans seemed confused by the information we had provided them. It was as if they knew nothing of the attack on the community. It was impossible for me to remember anyone answering that name. «Hecate». I was hoping that whomever she was, she could really save me and return my energy to the one it was before that fateful shot.

There came a time when I no longer listened to what was happening around me. I only noticed the cold touch of the human, which was gradually equal to the temperature of my body. I tried to expand my energy for the last time, but I didn't even scratch the surface of the hole where it had been hidden. I felt that it was still beating inside me, so I still had hope of saving myself. The leg cooled down at times and it was barely possible to move. I knew Bruce kept the weapon that had left me in that state. I hoped he would be able to use it in due time, if things were not going well. I felt a pang of pain as I imagined what was left of my family suffering from that martyrdom.

A voice tore the silence. And I felt how the energy quickly surrounded us. For an instant I thought I would not survive the trip, but I chose to let go and if that was to be my last union with the light of the world, I would enjoy knowing that I died with the human whom I never wanted to kill and knowing that our saviors would take good care of him.

The trip lasted longer than expected, but I got to see its end. I was exhausted, really sore and with the skin already as cold as the human.

"We have arrived, Ange," Bruce's voice was a consolation that for a few moments made me believe that nothing had happened. "Open your eyes."

An iridescent light burned my pupils. It was only two seconds until I could see the magnitude of the place we were in. It was a gigantic white room; of a burning white. The roof was so far away from us that, in my state, I could only guess the distance to which it was.

I took a look at my leg for the first time since the forest incident. It seemed to be fine. At first glance I might think it was healing slowly. But no, I knew it wasn't like that. In spite of its appearance, inside it was shattered; it had only regenerated the upper layer and little more of my armor. I would never be complete if my energy wasn't too.

I looked back at the environment where we were and I saw someone. A woman. I saw a woman approaching us, walking... no, she was floating. She had to be someone in the community!

"I did not expect a visit from a member of the Royal family!"

Her voice was too sharp. She had a slender body and a long blond mane, which came down to her knees. Her skin was not as white as mine, it was like Bruce's, with a more tanned tone; and her eyes, incredibly blue. There was no doubt: she belonged to our world.

"Who are you?" I managed to jabber.

"I am Hecate" She said and her voice was lifted with the wind. "The first one to take this world, after the True Great War."

What was she saying? I couldn't believe someone would have gotten back into this world before us. I looked around, there were a large number of humans with us, watching the meeting.

"How did you survive giving them so much of your energy?"

"The corn spikes are not ready until the farmer believes they are," it was the only thing she said.

At any other time, I would have been enraged; I may even have charged against her. But, now, I just wanted her to help me. I was going to beg her when, all of a sudden, Bruce came forward.

"Please!" He asked. "Help her!"

I lost my support when he ran to Hecate. He knelt at her feet and again he implored her to save me. I dropped to the ground, it made no sense to spend energy that could not regenerate. I tried to think of something nice, so it would be easier for me to die. It was my punishment for allowing Aingeru's death and also, for having rescued those two children who, condemned the community.

"Okay," that she accepted so well, surprised us both. "Stay very still if you don't want to experience another degree of pain!"

Another one, I thought. Could it be even worse? She stooped to my side and took my leg abruptly. I leaned with my elbows to raise my head and look at her.

"You've never felt what fear or pain is," she told me. "Right?" She caressed my skin with her fingertips. "It didn't take me long to experience all those difficult feelings. It was better when there were just us," her blue eyes were fixed on mine.

"That's why we're back." I managed to say.

She released an exclamation. An attempt of laughter that made it clear how little she liked our presence.

"How did this happen?" She asked, with her face disfigured by the surprise and the fear, after touching my leg with the open palm.

Bruce dedicated a meaningful look to me, I shook my head in denial. Hecate noticed the gesture.

"With this," Bruce said, taking the gun out of his pocket very slowly, despite my reluctance to show anyone such a contraption.

Now, if she was really able to save me, we would have to give her the weapon as payment; or if, on the contrary, she believed that she did not have to, she would simply take it and kill us.

"I don't get it," lamented Hecate. "A human weapon has left your leg like this?"

"Is not human," I managed to say. Since Bruce had sunk us more, why not getting to the bottom. "Help me and we'll tell you everything!"

Hecate pouted her lips, she wanted to seem annoyed for seeing herself in the need to make deals with me but, the truth was that she was delighted. A part of me was infuriated by being the mere entertainment of someone like her.

"It is ok!" She coiled up a lock of hair between her fingers. "Try not to shout... too much." She added with a laughter.

She didn't even give me time to understand what she was going to do to me. She introduced her hot hand into my leg. I felt the snap of my cold skin at her contact and the tearing of the muscles that no longer had salvation resounded in my head as if they were hitting me with a hammer. My body got tense with each of the times that she removed the hand and reintroduced it. I felt that my dead flesh bounced off the ground and I imagined the face that Bruce would have as he was seeing such a spectacle. I had closed my eyes and I used what was left of my energy in the hard work of not screaming.

That was a torture.

I should not be feeling all that; I should not hear my muscles splitting, as if they were branches; Nor should I be there, surrounded by humans and at the mercy of someone I knew nothing about. As the seconds went by, her fingers, scorching before, now came slowly to my temperature. Which means the heat in my body was regenerating.

I tried to concentrate again on my energy and on that occasion, I could release what I had repressed. I heard a slight creaking, which followed a strong explosion inside me. The energy ran through my body like a raging flow. I filled every fiber of my being with such a long-awaited feeling and for the first time, of what seemed to have been an eternity, I was me again.

I opened my eyes and found that the light was simply white; much less than what I had ever seen. Now it was all the same as it had always been. Perfect. I got up by a big jump. My muscles responded to the effort in a good way; I could feel how many humans were in the room and, indeed, I had an inner strength unfitting of their race. I was again in tune with all the creatures of that wonderful world; it was as if none of that had happened.

"I thank you," I told Hecate, bowing my body in her direction. "I don't know what would have become of me if you didn't show up."

She made a conceited smile.

"In fact," she corrected me. "It is you who have appeared," she turned around, which allowed me to observe the magnitude of her energy. She had a very strong and slender body; her curves were marked under the robe at each step. "Now," she continued, sitting in the air on an imaginary chair, "tell me what has happened to you, O great Queen of Heaven.

All the humans of her congregation gathered around us to hear our insane story. Hecate and Bob's gestures, which seemed to be her second, were twisted as I advanced, but they did not interrupt us. Bruce and I hadn't even moved from the place. I decided that it was best to start with the first time we had seen each other: I said I was the first to decide not to kill. I overlooked the robbery of the stone because, apart from not having meant anything to us, it had been erased from my mind. I did mention Bayron and Ribek, the traitors, and a shiver ran through my body. I didn't know yet how Bruce felt, his undaunted countenance told me nothing.

Hecate and Bob didn't take their eyes off the gun. I knew it wouldn't be long before we had to fight for it. A part of me wanted to have as far as possible that contraption but, at the same time, I didn't conceive the idea of having to separate from it.

We waited for our words to cause effect on their minds. Humans had created a murmur that burst out loud. However, there were two people who were not happy to have us so close. Hecate got up in a jump. Her long white dress got stuck to her body, at the same time that her hair lifted. I believed, for a moment, that she would attack us. There was no trace of the amusement that, just a moment ago, shone behind her face.

"Get out of here," she ordered. "Go away and don't come back."

However, such words confused us all.

Bob turned his face towards her, he was as surprised as we were. He said something in a low voice, but she did not even come to consider it. She walked with slow and measured pace towards us. Bruce looked at her with a mixture of admiration and fear; it was understandable, the energy that she gave off was like a lighthouse in the midst of a fog.

"You can't be serious!" I exploded. "You know what they've done." My voice sounded desperate. I was beginning to look like a human when he prays at the time of his death. Because if we were thrown out of there, there would be no salvation for us. "They have destroyed your people," I said, trying to appeal her sense of unity. "You have to help us…"

She burst into a guffaw, which more than laughter, denoted rage and madness.

"My people," she made a pause and added, "said the sweet princess." Her energy returned to a low point and I soon noticed that she was relaxing. "Those creatures which let me leave a prison alone, into this world."

I didn't understand what she was talking about.

Her humans shut up.

"Madam," Bob intervened. "We can't let them go. That would condemn them to death."

"Oh, don't talk nonsense!" Hecate smashed her hair against her head. "Only he will die." Bruce's face was a poem, he was even more frightened than I was. "She's immortal, remember?" She turned around and seemed to remember something, because she turned her head to look at us and the expression of her face did not bode well. "Unless... they shoot her again with that." She pointed at the contraption with her finger.

Bruce kept it in his jacket. As I had foreseen, she would take our gun and kill us both.

"I won't give it to you!"

"Oh, of course you will!" She howled, with the beautiful face disfigured by anger.

She reminded me of a demon of the stories that Bruce read in the library. I did not understand what was it that she intended to do with the weapon, but if for some reason we left that room, unprotected, we would have no chance it the Hunters found us.

"Princess," she called me, with a sweet voice. "Give me the contraption and you can stay here," her blue eyes shone in a sinister way. "I assure you."

She did not even wait for me to answer, as she spoke, she had realized how little believable she sounded. She pounced on Bruce, at such a speed that I could only see her. We collided violently, the blow was so strong and so powerful, that we were lifted several meters in the air by it. While I was holding her by both arms, I could see her raging expression... changing. She relaxed her body and we fell heavily in the center of the great stay. She got rid of me with a strong move, though anyway, I was no longer exerting pressure on her. She was a strange creature. She really was. In a second she was kind with all of us and in less than a flicker, she lost control. Although there was something in her energy that also changed with her mood; it would be impossible for me to grasp the real potential of her power.

"Listen," she said, at last. "Collect your belongings!" A murmur full of exclamations rose among her humans. "We have to leave before it's too late."

"Yes, ma'am," muttered the ones around us.

"Why are you running away?" I asked her, I needed to make her angry so she could understand that she should help us.

Her back was turned when I spoke. She had picked up the long mane, leaving the muscles of her neck uncovered, which got tense when she heard my words.

"Why?" She took both hands to his head, the sleeves of her dress slipped to reveal a drawing on the skin of her forearm. "You tell me an unreal and absurd story. I believe you," she closed her eyes for an instant. "If they have attacked first in your territory, it is because they want to govern," her mocking tone didn't go unnoticed. "And they won't stop until they find you," her gaze got fixed on Bruce. "Both of you" she corrected herself. "And I'm not going to jeopardize my community, just because of your ridiculous rivalries."

"Rivalries?" I burst. "He wants to kill us!"

"Do you not understand that in the same way that they don't care about me, I do not care about them either?"

I moved back several steps. It was clear that we were not going to get anything from her. What I felt for my community was the same that she felt for the new one she had created.

"Let's go, Bruce!" I ordered. I turned around and walked with a decisive step to the entrance. "Bruce!" I called him for a second time.

He walked hesitantly towards me, for he was watching Hecate putting on a great golden robe.

"Do you want me to take you?" I asked. "Now, I am helpful again."

He smiled at me tenderly.

"I hope we don't meet again with them," he kept the contraption in his trousers. "Maybe we can hide as well as these people do."

"Of course!" I passed my arm over his shoulder, I knew it was a gesture of affection and complicity that he would appreciate.

"Hold on!" Shouted Bob's loud voice, which resounded all over the room. It was followed by a thundering silence. "I'll go with you," If I had more emotional capacity, my mouth would also have opened the same way as Bruce did.

"What are you saying, human?" Hecate exploded. Her bun of hair had vanished being replaced by a large mass of bristling blond hair. Something was not working right with her, I was more certain as time passed by. "You can't..." her voice faltered, "abandon me."

Bob looked at her. He walked towards her slowly. He was a pretty big, tall human. If it were not for the strange energy emanating from Hecate, I would have said that she was the human. Bob took one of her hands in both his hands, delicately. And a great halo of energy surrounded them both; an energy that I had never seen, or only vaguely remembered.

"You can't abandon them either." The tension of the moment was getting heavier and heavier. "I'm going to go with them because that's the right thing. You can stay here or find a new home for everyone," he dropped Hecate's hand free, who took several moments to feel that her hand was no longer being covered by her partner's embrace and slid it languidly until it found her leg, "or come with us and stop the beginning of another catastrophe."

The strange creature's face got twisted. A large black cloud rose from his feet to cover it almost entirely. I placed Bruce on my back, for such a damaging energy could even kill him.

"All right, human!" She turned on herself and sat on the great throne created on the basis of smoky energy. "If that's your decision," she closed her eyes and a big red flash lit her forehead, I wondered if Bruce could see what I was seeing. "Get out with those two death heralds! And whomever wants to leave with them" she added; "whomever wants to have the worst of deaths", she gave a brief glance to all her followers, "they can also leave."

The humans hesitated for a moment. I knew that no one would come with us, for although their energy had been altered by that of Hecate, they would never cease to be what they are and none of them would leave the security that she offered them, for helping us. And to prove me right, not even two seconds have passed by for them to put their knees on the ground, to show their dear lady who they were with.

Hecate smiled.

"Let's go, guys," whispered Bob, crestfallen.

All the hardness that had detached his face, even the strength emanating from him was fading, slowly.

"If you pass through the doors of our territory," said Hecate, with a cold tone that hit against my energy, "you'll be a mere human again."

Perhaps I hoped that in the prospect of losing the energy that gave him more vitality, he would remain at her side.

"All right, my lady," he accepted. "After all, it's who I am. A mere human," his gaze was of pure pain. There was something I was not able to understand in everything I saw.

We walked quietly to the door. I felt that I was passing through a thin transparent layer of gelatin and a great relief to feel that outside, in that thick forest in which we were, energy flowed within me stronger; but Bob did not seem so relieved: he staggered as soon as he crossed the threshold. Bruce hurried to hold him.

"Are you ok?" he asked him kindly.

"Yes," he said, without much conviction. "I didn't remember it felt this way."

I watched Bruce holding the human and felt slightly guilty, for letting him carry his weight alone. So, I activated my armor to the full, so that I would not be so disinclined to touch the other.

"Now what?" They asked me in unison, when I approached to help.

I don't know if it bothered me or I was pleased to be allowed to choose.

"For now," my voice sounded far away, "let's get away from this place."

I believed for a second that we would succeed in getting away and leave Hecate and her rejection in oblivion; I thought we would never see her again and that we would really get to do something to stop the two traitors. For a second I thought it was possible.

Bruce and Bob screamed when the explosion burst on our back, they lost their balance and fell to the ground. I stood up steady. Something inside me, before turning around and watching what had happened, was already giving me the devastating image. «The worst of deaths», just as Hecate had said. The image of her red lips struck my mind and guilt clutched my belly. If someone had died, it would have been our fault.

"Let's go!" I urged the humans. "We have to go back."

They were so slow... why didn't they move more quickly, now that I was already recovered? The fastest way to get to and through the smoke that covered the area where their hideout was, was to go through it all with the light. I took them both by the waist; their hearts were pounding and they were clinging to me as if I was their only lifesaver in an enraged sea. I felt a small spark of energy inside me and even without having checked the state I was in, I transported with the humans to the place where Hecate had saved me.

The trip was short, maybe with a longer one we would have had problems. When the smoke that covered the whole room was dissipated, we saw more clearly what had happened: the scorched bodies were visible everywhere, hundreds of smoky skeletons, some of them, dismembered, throughout the room.

Bayron was there, wrapped in smoke and in an aura of burning power. He had full armor, which shone with the menacing radiance of the purple stone; the arm he held in the air was covered with a yellow energy, responsible for burning everything. Hecate was in the center of the great hall, her inexpressive gaze indicated that she had not yet managed to assimilate anything that was happening; inside of her, it was not possible that the whole community had vanished without a trace. All in a matter of seconds.

"Let's hide!" Urged Bob. "I'm sure he hasn't seen us."

The traitor turned around towards us, Hecate had passed to a second level. The human had had a brilliant idea however, he forgot an important detail: my energy was indeed important to him. At the instant that our eyes crossed, I relived the pain that clutched me inside and an icy path on my cheek was drawn again. Bayron gave a dull laughter. His gaze was fixed on me, so Bruce and Bob managed to get to Hecate without any problems. I was not afraid, I repeated myself.

"How pleasing it is," he began to say, barely moving from the place he was, "to see you so well!"

He walked to get near me, his shadow covered me completely. I knew I was stronger and that if I could only wait for Hecate to react, it would all be over. But I found myself paralyzed by the fear of feeling that again. He was a great mass of metal that could hide a weapon like the one that had led me almost to death.

"You wouldn't be anything without that armor." I repeated to him, trying to destabilize him. He fully stopped. "You're just a traitor. A traitor who allies with humans, to rise up against his own race."

"Are you accusing me of allying with humans?" His voice was soft and devious, though I saw that he found it amusing. "It's so absurd!" He released a laughter. "You saved them!" He raised his arms, evoking a moment that got withered in my memory. You can't accuse me of anything, because they're all dead because of you."

It was a hard blow to me. No doubt that was the base of the vine growing around both: the death of loved ones. Sometimes I wonder, if there was anything, even if only for a short moment of our existence, that I could have done to change our destinies; but I'm sure nothing would have untied our lives.

"What have you done with my family?" I asked, even though I knew he was not going to answer me.

Bruce and Bob hadn't gotten Hecate to come back to herself. The blow she had suffered had transported her mind to a very distant place, to which we had no access.

"Come with me and you'll see," that answer, however, overwhelmed me. I receded several steps, losing ground. "Come both with me."

His eyes shone through the hull. I knew that proposal wouldn't last long. He would soon yield to anger and if I could only take advantage of making him losing control of the situation, I would achieve to get us all alive from there, because there was something that was clear to me and it was that if we were caught by him, we would all be lost.

"Go with you?" I couldn't help but to put my arms in front of myself, fearing that he would get too close. "The only way we could travel together" I knew the coup would soon come, "is to hold your head on a pike."

Filled with rage, he landed a violent blow, which I easily dodged. His calm attitude had changed radically, he was not able to control the blows, nor to anticipate that I would be able to jump before he reached me. Now he was an uncontrolled beast, who no longer knew against whom he charged. What more could be expected from a traitor? I released a laughter to make him more nervous. At the time when he seemed already about to lose the little sense that remained in him, Bob shouted Hecate's name strong enough for Bayron to take him for an easier target, but not enough for her to recover self-control. The Hunter ran to them. I was at the top of the great hall and I also did the same to get there before him. I felt our bodies grazed and the magnetic field of his armor reacted with mine; I had just enough time to push Bruce away from the traitor's trajectory. I raised my head, hoping to see that Hecate would have done the same with her human, but no; what I saw was Bayron holding Bob's neck. He was determined to kill the last two humans that were close. The horror that Bruce reflected in his gaze made me remind him of what we should do.

"We have to escape," I told him. "Let's go now that he's entertained with the other human!"

My desperation, and my fear of losing Bruce was talking. I had not stopped to think that, I was beginning to worry too much about some humans' welfare. I rose from a jump, but something stopped me; it was Bruce's hand. He did not want to leave them, after all, we were to blame that they had ended like this. He was right, we couldn't leave.

"You guys are phonies!" Howled Bayron to heaven, lifting his left arm and going through Bob's chest. "You should have never been created."

The following moments were marked by something I have not seen in another creature except in her. Bruce was screaming and was about to lose consciousness, it was his first dead human. Bob's body laid on the floor, breathing for the last time. When I wanted to approach him, I saw that Hecate came to herself and the expression of her face did not bode well. Bayron had lost control way before, and now she made it clear that she had long lost it. From her disfigured mouth came a shocking shout, which made Bruce shrink like a ball.

"Bastard!"

His blond mane fluttered over his head as if it was being protected by a yellow bird. He raised his arms; the drawings began to shine and in less than an instant he fired a brutal blue ray on the Hunter. Despite the great impact he could only move him for several meters.

"I'll rip your soul out!" Bayron was beginning to charge for his coup, "If you have one left..."

Maybe if Bob hadn't been deathly wounded, Hecate wouldn't have used so much power. But the pain of her loss had led to the extreme of spending all her energy on that first and apparently, only blow. Bayron had also noticed, his opponent had controlled the battle badly and now she was also dead. He smiled. Hecate didn't move and as if we were imagining it, the blue glow came out from her again. I couldn't believe she would have recovered so quickly. Something was different about her. Certainly! Something I hadn't seen in anyone. Her blows were getting better, stronger and more lethal.

"Bob" I heard someone whispered, "hold on."

It was Bruce's voice. He had approached the dying man, no matter what was going on just a few meters from him. He just wanted to cheer him up. I didn't know what to do. I was paralyzed. Should I help the human or Hecate? I decided to help the human, for it did not seem that Bayron was a problem for her.

"He's losing a lot of blood," I told Bruce, who looked at me reproachfully.

What had I said? I thought. We heard an explosion that forced the three of us to raise our heads. It was Bayron, which was lost in the depths of the sky. Hecate descended in a sigh to our place.

"Oh, how sorry I am!" She mumbled, stroking his chin. "I shouldn't have taken it away from you."

Bob laughed.

"We had been postponing it for many years."

How old would that human be? I knew immediately that Bruce would also be wondering that. We became mere spectators of the massacre we had provoked.

Bob coughed and stained Hecate's white robe with blood. What was happening between them? I wondered. Why did I seem to be the only one who didn't know what was going on? Even Bruce, having been able to see the energy that was created around him, would know what I wondered, though looking into his eyes, I knew he didn't need to see what I saw, to know.

"We're going to beat it one more year," implored the sweet voice of Hecate.

She rested his head on her lap, oblivious to everything else. She pulled her sleeve backwards and left the black drawings uncovered. They had a convoluted form that would certainly mean something. Bob let out a sigh, he wouldn't have much time. The wound that Bayron had inflicted on him formed a large puddle on the ground. The damage was irreparable. Bruce was acquiring a blue color, he was trying not to vomit.

Hecate bit her arm and a strange blood-like fluid sprouted from it. Now, who was about to vomit was me: what was that? She approached her arm into her human's mouth. As Bob drank from Hecate's arm, Bruce staggered until he had to lean on me. Which I thanked, for I began to think that everything was a kind of dream.

Bob's blood did not return to its place, it remained shed on the ground. But what I did see was that, little by little, he regained vitality. Whatever was that he was drinking, was leaving a black furrow on Hecate's skin. And it was at that very moment that I understood everything: the community of humans; the strange glow with which they shone; their unity and the shock that she had suffered by seeing them dead. She had given them a part of herself so that none would die, so that they would remain at her side until the end of time. She had given them the greatest blessing that can be given to a human: our power. And that's why she had felt the pain of each of their deaths.

But with this human in particular, it was different. I knew it in some way: in her way of holding his head; in her reaction to Bayron's attack; on how her skin was sticking to the bones, because of giving up so much of her energy.

"That's enough." I intervened.

Hecate opened her eyes. And they were just two blue dots inside a black basin. So much was the energy that she had given to him? Bob's shirt was still stained with blood, but his wound was no longer there. I did not know whether her energy had rebuilt his body, or whether it had given him new organs. The idea of keeping Bruce alive that way went, swiftly, through my mind.

Hecate got up first. Her arm was stained with that strange liquid, which had formed a new drawing.

"This, princess," she said, raising her arm. There were still drops that had not been transformed into a figure, "is the materialization of our energy. The energy that we all possess."

"Why does it burn your skin?" I asked, without trusting her, "Why doesn't it come back to you?"

Hecate laughed and that time it didn't look like she was mocking me.

"There are so many things to learn," she raised her head to heaven, the moonlight bathed her face, "when you are in an unknown world."

"You can't do that forever," in reality, it was jealousy and fear to the unknown, what was talking in my behalf. "It's not right to keep something alive, that must die," they hadn't even listened to me. Bruce was too busy trying to stand up and they seemed to have a mental conversation. Angry, I shouted: "how long do you think you'll go on with this?"

They separated and took each other's hands. Hecate's arms were covered again by the bloody robe's sleeve.

"Everything has a price," a drop of energy impacted the ground. "Even for us," the drop was transformed into a beautiful plant; a plant that brought me a sweet memory. "I will stop doing so on the day when there is nothing left inside of me that keeps me clinging to this life," I didn't remember the name of the flower, but Bruce had given it to me the day we met. "And that day is approaching swiftly. Don't you see?" She asked me and then I remembered the name of the flower. "I'm dying."

A rose. The flower that Bruce gave me was a rose.

Chapter 8

«The Titans' True Appearance»

Kill. Eat. Drink. Hunt. Kill. And kill... and eat. What's going on? I don't know. I do not know what is in my hands but, there is something that I have very clear indeed: now I am invincible. I see a new colorful light everywhere, a soft caress, as sweet as a kiss.

It's time! They're waiting for me! They do not know but... they are waiting for me. The smell they give off is almost as pleasant as the memory of their blood in my throat.

Fragment of Hecate's lost diary.

"Now what?" Bruce asked aloud.

"Now what?" repeated Hecate, with a pouting of disdain? "You destroy my house and that's the only thing you ask me?"

"Are you going repeat the same thing all day? We've been for hours," he told me lengthening the word, "walking and you've done nothing but to blame us!"

"Because it is your fault, human!"

"Don't say it like it's an insult!"

That's how they've been since Bruce woke up. A whole morning of complaints on both sides. Hecate liked to have someone to vent her frustration and so did Bruce. But what seemed like a simple quarrel, soon became something more personal. I walked at the lead, trying to be as far away as possible from their cries; Bob, on his part, did what he could to keep up with me. He had strong legs and as the terrain became more difficult, his heart changed pace and got adapted, not like Bruce's. It was hard for him to follow our step and even more if he put all his energy into arguing with Hecate.

I threw my head back, to see how they were going. Finally, a little peace of mind. Hecate's sleeves were entangled in the branches of the bushes which we passed by and I noticed that several tiny insects had already been installed in her hair. None of those details seemed to bother her. During those moments when they were silent, she seemed to be in another dimension, far away from us; and the same thing happened with Bruce, however, he did not seem to be absorbed, his gaze was lost due to the effort he was making. I turned around, to help him climb, then he stumbled and after a cry, accompanied by a crunch, he fell to the ground as long as he was.

"You broke my robe!"

"Can't you see I've fallen?" Bruce got up with difficulty, "Oh! I've cut myself..."

Hecate receded, incredibly frightened by the blood of Bruce's hands.

"Shit..." mumbled Bob, standing in the way between us and her.

I took Bruce's hands, delicately, those were just scratches, nothing to worry about. I smiled and helped him get up.

"It's nothing," he also had a pitiful look, like Hecate. They seemed to have come out of the same dunghill.

I looked at her, she was still in shock. She didn't look away from Bruce's hands. I hoped she would not begin to utter insults for shattering her robe.

"Come on, ma'am," intervened, Bob. "We have to rest," I didn't know if he was addressing me or her. "I'm going to take the boy to fetch food," she sat calmly on the floor, her tunic was torn and stained in blood. "We'll be back right after dark," he informed me, very earnestly. "You watch her."

Watch her? Who did he think he was talking to? I saw that Bruce was thrilled at the prospect of doing something for himself. I sighed and agreed to stay by her side.

I watched her for a few moments: under the soft light of dusk, her blond hair shone, all she was a glittering ball; except for those two black dots she had as eyes, which were all pupil. I felt shocked; it was too much, in such a short time. A betrayal. A flee. A wound. The pain. The loss of my power. And finding her. My leg began to tingle, which made me fear a subsequent pain.

However, nothing happened.

Hecate smiled at me.

I buried my face in my hands when the darkness of a new night fell on us, telling myself that I could not contact my father for another day.

"Your father is not yet dead," she said it in a soft voice, as if she just claimed that the moon came out at night, as if it were nothing serious.

"Now, you know that?" I turned my back on her, hoping she would decide to end the conversation.

I tried to get all kinds of meaningless images out of my mind, about what I thought could be happening to my father.

"Yes..." said Hecate, scratching the floor with her hands. "Now."

I turned the face to look at her, she seemed sorry. She had curled up herself in a ball by the trunk of a tree, she looked smaller than she really was. I raised my head to the sky, trying to guess the distance to which all those stars were.

"It's always like this," she went on, talking as low as if I wasn't there. "When they want something bigger, they take one thing you love," maybe it was because of the tone or the words, but I started to turn around, "they make you think they're going to destroy that thing," she seemed to be remembering, "and then, when the deal they wanted is signed..." She stood on her knees, to be nearer to me.

"So that's when you get that you love?" I asked, imagining that my father was safe.

"No," all my hope was fading away. "It is then when they take away everything," she took my hands vehemently. "When they take away everything and show their true intentions!"

"I'll fight them!" I snapped. "I don't need any deal!"

She sat down again against the trunk.

"Your father will want to see you before make any deals."

Something in me broke, understanding that I would not be the one to close any deal; something in me stopped working, when I realized that it was me the only thing that was missing to do that deal. I was that thing he loved.

"That's why he came looking for us..." I mumbled, horrified. "I don't know what that monster asked for, but...!"

"He can't catch you before you talk to your father."

"Nor Bruce! Because if they have him..."

"... They got you."

Everything was staggering again. I had to find a way to get in touch with him before Bayron got whatever he was plotting.

"You know?" added Hecate. "When I told you that you were a princess, I meant it. You can't conquer a kingdom playing fair. Your father must think that he has you in his power, besides, he may also be hurt and without having someone like me..."

"The pain!"

I had to lean against a log, I remembered Bruce vomiting and I laughed nervously. If my father was suffering that torment, just waiting to know how I was...

"Don't worry," she whispered in my ear, she passed her arms around my waist and carefully dropped her head on my back. "Now you have me."

I was paralyzed by fear. All the problems she had had, had been our fault, even that scary past she had with our community. Her humans were dead; Bob almost died; she herself, was on the verge of a terrible death in the hands of Bayron. I sighed. I didn't understand why she wanted to help us.

"I'm going to bring the kids back," she communicated me, turning away from me. I dropped to the ground, without moving my hands from the trunk, "before they hurt themselves."

It was the last time, at least that long night, that I saw her being herself. Because what came next was a nightmare, a horror that transformed into a terrible burning sea.

I was lying on the floor, suddenly my legs were not responding. Knowing that my father was suffering, not just an attack, but the anguish of believing that I was going through the same thing, made me feel weak. Even knowing that it would be useless, I tried to contact him. My energy hit squarely against an impenetrable wall.

"I'll get there," I promised to the wind. "I'll be there in time."

I soon recovered and began to notice that it had been a long time since Hecate had left. I wasn't going through a proper time to tolerate waiting. When I was going to extend my energy to locate Bruce, I heard something moving in the bushes. It could be anything: Bruce, Bob or Hecate... or some other threat. My fear began to vaporize the puddles of water and being about to throw a blind blow, in the direction of the alleged threat, I saw that it was Bruce.

"Hey!" The light of my hand got extinguished instantly. "Why are you alone?"

"I don't know!" He was very upset. He had been running in the shadows for a long time. "I was with Bob and he was teaching me how to set a trap and then...!"

"Then what?" I tried not to look too anxious but I didn't get it.

"That demon came," that's all I could have imagined. "But she looked like..."

"What did she look like, Bruce?"

"I'm not sure," he scratched his head with a trembling hand. "She looked like someone else," I wanted to interrupt, to say that she wasn't a person, but I kept quiet. "And she looked sick. She stumbled upon a branch and when Bob went to help her, her face... it scared me," he concluded.

"And you ran away."

"And I ran away," I attracted him to me, carefully, seeing how my fears were fed by endless nightmares. "Those black eyes weren't the ones that looked at us the first time."

"Come, let's go."

Now we had two problems that either tried to kill us or do something worse.

We walked in silence for a long time. Bruce noticed that there was something that worried me and luckily, seeing such empty eyes so close, kept him quiet. I wasn't trying to move in a stealthy way; why, she would find us anyway? Bruce's footsteps were silent, he hoped not to see those terrible eyes again, so he strove to make no noise and to leave no trace. I didn't mean to tell him that no matter what he did or how hard he strove, she would always find us.

I had a feeling that nothing, absolutely nothing was chasing us. If I had felt at that moment a pair of eyes lurking from the gloom, perhaps I would have reassured myself, because the anguish of not feeling anything was worse.

We stopped an instant before putting our feet in a glade bathed by the moonlight. I was evaluating the idea of crossing it or going around it when I heard Bruce's tremulous voice.

"Let's not go that way," he whispered. "I'm sure it's a trap."

A trap, I thought. Yes, it was clear it could be. Everything could be a trap. Tired, I took a moment to look at Bruce. He had lost a lot of weight since our escape; his eye sockets were beginning to sink; his blond hair was so dirty that it still had ashes from the explosion. I wanted to arrive soon to any place in which we could rest.

"Never mind," his face shrank into a grimace of concern. "We have to get out of here and find water and food for you."

He seemed to recognize the need, for the first time. We had spent already several days moving away from home and deterioration in Bruce was evident.

We advanced through the glade with caution. I took Bruce's hand, hoping to get out of the woods without any setback. The moon bathed us with its light when we walked through the glade, I slowly turned the head, towards the place where Bruce's shadow was projected: a silhouette trimmed in the grass, which was extending its hand to hold nothing...

If we were in the world of shadows, he would be alone.

"Maybe someday you'll get one."

"Yes," I said. "Maybe someday."

A small cloud left us an instant in the gloom and as it cleared up, we saw her silhouette. A twisted body covered with a robe that was already tattered. She looked at us for a long time, as if we weren't there.

"It's..." began to say Bruce. Hecate resumed the march. She went through the edge of the forest and disappeared into the thicket. "Was that blood?"

The tone of preoccupation in his voice made me hesitate momentarily, but I pushed that thought away from my mind.

"Let's go get her!"

"What? No!" I understood the fear that he felt, however, the need to understand what was happening to her was stronger.

"It's okay!" I cried out, pulling him to where she had gone. "Where would Bob be?" that issue triggered something in his mind, as he stopped pulling back. "Do you think she had hurt him?"

"Of course not!"

Although he swallowed saliva.

When the branches and leaves took us away from the bright light, I felt that we entered in the mouth of an angry animal.

I heard something a few steps beyond. I conducted us in that direction, hoping not to see the mutilated body of that human.

"It's her," mumbled Bruce.

Bruce approached carefully. I approached slowly, fearing anything that might happen to him.

"Hey..." He began to tell her. "What have you got there?"

She turned her back on us, she was convulsing as she squeezed something in her hands. She threw her head back, her tangled hair slipped like a snake and for an instant made me feel that it wasn't her.

"Bruce," I began to say, "no..."

She left something on the floor and the sound of her feet as she slipped over the leaves, made us shudder. We recoiled a few steps but, Bruce had already extended his hand forward, ignoring all that was to come...

"No!" I achieved to scream.

The atmosphere was filled with the smell of Bruce's blood and with his shouts. He was struggling to take her off him, but she was too strong. I wanted to throw a ball of energy, but fearing that might hit Bruce, I restrained myself to hit her in the head, which sent her some meters away. She took her head out of the bushes, showing us a bloody smile.

Bruce was crying, trying to stop the bleeding. He staggered until he laid on the ground.

"What have you done?"

I covered his wound with both hands, trying to stop the blood stream, but it was useless.

"Is..." she began to say.

"Bob!" I shouted, hoping to be able to take care of Bruce, while someone stopped her.

"It hurts!" Bruce clung tightly to my shoulders. "It hurts so much!"

I took Bruce gently and leaned him against a tree. I called Bob again, I shouted his name to the shadows, but nothing happened.

"That smell! That smell!" She kept on humming. "It is so..."

"Hecate, stop it!" It was the first time I used her name to refer to her. "We can..." I approached her, with my hands up, "fix it."

She released a gloomy laughter.

"Fix..." she took a hand to her face. "It cannot be fixed," as she spoke, the tone of her voice was acquiring a threatening tone, "what is not broken."

Like a lightning, she pounced upon me, her face disfigured. I held the blow, grabbing her by the wrists. I wanted to hurt her; I wanted to punish her for having hurt Bruce but, I remembered how she had gotten rid of Bayron and I would need all my energy to defeat her and at that moment, I was more concerned about not hurting Bruce (who kept on lamenting on the ground), than about such a brutal fight. Because that would certainly be what she would give me. I had to get rid of her and leave there with Bruce. Hecate was frantic and she wasn't even putting all her effort with me. She surely had killed Bob.

I spun around several times, forcing her to follow me in the twist. If I managed to destabilize her and throw her against the trees, we could run away and leave her behind forever. When it seemed that I could not let her go and that we would be in that crazy dance through all eternity, fate wanted to smile to us, causing one of her feet to get entangled in a root; I took advantage of her oversight to throw her as far as I could from Bruce. It wasn't much, I regretted it. Hecate weighed a lot. It was like moving a mountain, with the mere force of the breeze. She was not focused on me, I noticed it in her way of falling. Her mind was not in the fight, not even on Bruce... Something had transported her away from there. She remained lying on the floor, indifferent. I receded several steps towards Bruce.

If she really wanted to turn me away to kill him, she could have done it with just one move. At that time, I was no match for her, I wanted to convince myself that it was because I had half of my energy put in the human and it was then, when I turned the face in her direction, in which I observed our great advantage: I saw it shine in Bruce's jacket, with the force of a lighthouse.

"Bruce!" I urged him. He looked at me, contrite. "Throw it at me!"

He let go of his wounded hand and took the weapon with difficulty, he threw it without much strength. I rushed to her, dreading to feel on the back Hecate's brutal blow. But nothing happened. I was paralyzed, holding the weapon that had done so much damage to me. My thigh was stiff and I began to feel a stream running from top to bottom. Was I going to shoot Hecate? Was I going to give her that pain? I swallowed saliva; my hands trembled when she got up and fixed her eyes into mine. An animal look.

"Don't move!" I threatened. Bruce crawled behind me. "Don't move!" I repeated.

"Let's go!" I heard him sobbing. "Come on!" He urged, pulling me.

"Yes, we're leaving..." I hesitated. "Stay away!"

She licked her lips, but the dried blood remained in place.

"You are leaving..." she whispered. "And you take him with you"

Her face was distorted in a grimace of rage.

"I don't want to shoot."

It was true. I didn't want to hurt her; I could not bear the idea of making her go through that hell. However, the danger that was looming in her eyes, already obscured by madness, made me lift the arms that pointed instinctively to her head. It's either her or us, I said, trying to convince myself. Her twisted body remained static, while I pointed at her; her gaze challenged me in an even more insane way than usual. Was she convinced I wouldn't shoot? No. She didn't know and there it was what she liked. Her game would never end.

I felt Bruce crouching beside me, ready to flee as soon as the shot sounded; I heard the drops of blood falling against the ground, so dark that it seemed to fade at our feet. I put my fingers on the trigger, and as I remembered seeing Bayron and Ribek, imagining that this would be how the mechanism was activated. A stream passed through my fingers again.

"I'm sorry," I tried to say, while I was gently pressing my fingers. I tried to look away but, instantly, I knew it wasn't a good idea. I had to keep it under control at all times.

"No!" Howled a voice from the brush. "Don't do it!" Bob's badly wounded body stood between both of us. "Please..."

It was at that very moment, that I realized what I was about to do. I let out an exclamation and dropped the gun to the ground.

"I..."

"I'm sorry," he stopped me. "I'm so sorry," I noticed his appearance, he seemed to have come out of a fight. "She's not like that, I swear."

Blood flowed from one of his shoulders.

"What happened to you?" I snapped, desiring to have the gun still in my hands.

Bruce stretched an arm to keep it.

"Shut up!" Hecate stood up straight at his side. She passed a blackened hand upon his arm. "Hush, my dear. Don't talk to them. I'm not finished yet."

"Oh, yes, we're done!" I claimed.

She released a laughter.

"I like you. I really like you," she took her hand to her nose, evoking the taste of Bruce. "I wanted to be with you all the way, but I changed my mind," her sharp-toothed smile eclipsed the night. "Now, all I want is to feel your life going through my throat."

Bruce hid behind me.

"I'll never allow it to you!"

"Or better..." She hesitated, looking at Bob. "We're going to keep on playing."

"Madam, No!" mumbled Bob.

She shut him up with a gesture.

"I don't want to hurt you again," she mumbled, taking his hand in hers. "Stay away until tomorrow!"

"You're a demon!" Bruce roared. "We should have killed you!"

"Yes," she conceded. "You should have done it. Now, there is only one option for you," she raised a hand, up to the height of her head: "run and die."

I took Bruce by one arm, when the first ball of green fire hit the ground. I ran through the woods, watching that gloomy glow and knowing that she hadn't missed the shot.

"Fly, you little birds! Fly! It's going to be dinnertime soon!"

Chapter 9

«Entrance to the Submerged City»

I'm going to throw this diary into the sea. No one is going to share anything I've suffered, so there's no point in saving it anymore. When I throw it into the sea, that monster can devour the last remaining of me, from now on I adopt a new name, I stop being a goddess and I become mortal. I can only hope that this falsehood gives me something more than these impostors, who only crave a little power to stand out over the rest.

Fragment of Hecate's lost diary.

I grabbed Bruce tight and I disappeared into the air. A current took us away from them and left us in a sheltered place, similar to the cave in which we hid for the first time. A part of me had wished for something like this to happen, from the very moment I knew of its existence.

I looked at Bruce, who had strayed from the entrance and was finding hard to breathe, however, he did not seem frightened at all. Such was his confidence in me? It's a good thing that one of us feared nothing, that would help me to try and see what I had to do. We could no longer use Hecate against Bayron, because she had gone mad; nor could we wait for him to come and fetch us, for he would kill us; but we neither could stay waiting for everyone to tear us apart. We had to do something soon.

I was terrified. My mind was still not able to process that emotion, but I really was. I remained at the entrance, fearing to lose control at any moment. Bruce came up to me. His face showed concern. I was losing confidence that we could come out well of that. Now I did see my frightened face reflected in his.

"Let's go to a city!" He said, in a trembling voice. His little body quivered beside me, it was too cold.

"There are no cities," I reminded him. I turned away from him and sat down on the floor, heavily. I rested my back on the wall and saw his figure trimmed against the sky, with soft shades of light not indicating that it was only a few hours before dawn. "We destroyed them all after the battle."

"Oh, come on!" He protested. He leaned over himself and began to draw something with the fingertip.

I allowed myself a loss of energy for him not to suffer the cold. After feeling it in his body, he smiled at me. I forgot a moment that there were so many people trying to kill us; I forgot the chaos and pain that tormented me and I enjoyed the vision that Bruce offered me: his hair had grown so much that it almost covered his eyes; the clothes, tattered, were glued to the body due to the dirt. The truth was that he offered a terrible image. When all that would come to an end and we were safe, at home, he would look radiant again. Suddenly, as if something had pushed him, he looked up until he could find my eyes.

"I had forgotten what you are," he said, erasing with his hand what he had done. "I had forgotten it until..." He looked away, uncomfortable.

"Until what?" I insisted. Bruce was looking at the floor. I was worried to see him grieving for his thoughts.

I got up slowly. I felt the whole weight of my body, as if I hadn't moved in years. I was hoping that the damage caused by that shot would not remain forever and that I could soon enjoy all the control of my power.

The light of dawn began to come out, it surrounded Bruce with a shining halo and left his face in shadows.

"She..." He took his wounded hand to the chest. "She reminds me of what you are."

I swallowed saliva and approached more.

"And what am I?" I asked, stooping at his side.

A murderer, I thought. A killing machine that was only stopped by an inhuman glow, a light that condemned us all.

Bruce opened his mouth to say something, but the words didn't get out of him. He threw his head to one side, frustrated. He fixed his eyes in mine, he never dared to do it that way. He took one of my hands in his, so delicately that it seemed a sigh. And at that moment, I forgot that Bruce belonged to the sub-race; I forgot he wasn't like me. At the bottom of his warm dark eyes, a secluded place shone brightly, in which he waited with hope that everything would end and we could be happy; I knew that in that place of his mind, there was a room for me —and I would fight against anything, whether it was a god or a demon, to keep him safe.

"You're my savior. You are my mother, my sister, my friend... My family."

I smiled. I was overwhelmed by a sense of peace that I would not have wanted to see broken by anything. It was a gentle caress that reached my soul. He wasn't afraid of me. I stretched out my hand to get him up and when he did, he lost his balance completely, rushing down the hillside.

"Bruce!"

I jumped and landed hard, raising dust from the ground, which dirtied my boots for a few moments. I saw him a few meters from me, lying face down. He was gradually sitting up and he indicated me with his hand to calm me down. Only he would be able to fall in that way.

"You must be more careful." I gave him a hand again, fully aware of the eyes that would be placed on us.

"I can get up by myself!" That's what he said.

He had hurt himself, but he wanted to disguise it, as if I had not noticed it already. He made all the noise he could, perhaps he would have forgotten that Hecate was chasing us; or maybe he didn't care anymore.

"Let's go!"

Although Bruce insisted on walking on his own and that could only mean that would be so slowed down, that they would capture us. Surely, that sudden eagerness meant that he wanted to prove himself that he could live without me. Perhaps, seeing that Bob enjoyed Hecate's vital energy, made him believe he was a hindrance. I sighed. That way of traveling only forced me to increase the level of alert. I didn't want Hecate to attack us while we were still on the ground.

I accelerated the step so that he would get tired as soon as possible and we could adopt a rhythm that would allow us to get out alive from that. I listened to him gasping at my back, trying to keep up. It took him several minutes to fall to the ground, asking me to stop. His face was red and swollen.

"I can't anymore," he admitted. "You won."

We went up to the trees again, everything seemed easier when the only thing we had on the head was the sky... the clouds, the stars and dim green flares, that were lost in the depths of the forest. I felt a sting in my head, so brief that, I thought I imagined it.

"It's moving away," mumbled Bruce.

He's just playing, I thought, even though I didn't tell him. He was focusing on the movements of the green light and I was not even able to lose sight of those bright dots, which were lost in the depths of the universe. Maybe that was the place we had escaped from. I no longer remembered.

We continued our journey, thinking that, at any moment, another of those fireballs would explode nearby and something told me that it would hit the target this time. At that moment, the only thing that made me believe that we would escape from her was the hope that Bruce's quick breath gave me.

I jumped to a bigger branch, one that could bear our weights. Something pulled me to the ground, but I did not want to attach importance to that, although it also did not allow me to continue straight. I just changed direction.

I heard a distant click, a sound that was gaining strength as it approached us. I managed to dodge that fireball, with hardly a margin of reaction. I felt the terror seized a part of my mind, I waited, in tension, to the next attack. It was going to be hard to get out of there, even more having to protect Bruce from all of that.

"She is not going to catch us, right?"

I noticed his heart beating me from all directions.

"No! She won't catch us!"

Although I was not sure at all about it. I remembered Hecate's bloodied face and Bruce's shouts, I couldn't let it happen again. Another ball of fire collided to our right, leaving what had once been a great tree, turned to ashes. We ran for a few minutes, trying to dodge the attacks, until I noticed something, she was marking us the way.

We were in another of her games but, I wasn't going to let her have fun with us that way.

"Why do we stop?" Bruce asked me, terrified. He couldn't even open his eyes. He was pale and sweaty. He did not seem very sure of our success, though, of course, how would he be, if they had tried to kill us three times.

The dense silence of the forest preceded the great storm that comes after the calm. She drove us to the West, I didn't know if it would be out of the woods or more inside it, but I wouldn't go to her trap willingly.

"Because if we're going to play," I turned around, ready to run, "it won't be under her rules."

I took what was left of my power to wrap us both. Almost at the same time we started to run, one of her fireballs exploded right before us but, we kept running, I stretched out to Bruce's hand, so that he wouldn't stay behind and we went through it without suffering any damage. There was no time to check the status of our bodies, because Hecate insisted on marking our way. If she didn't want us to go around there, it meant we were just heading in the right direction. I didn't even wonder what kind of trap she had ready for us. No. I just wanted to leave her behind.

I watched Bruce for a moment, it seemed that the race would have managed to keep him away from the pain of his hand. The reflection of the green rays made him acquire a more vital look. During that brief moment of my existence, running through the forest with Bruce, I felt it was the most real thing I had ever had. The most important thing. His tufts of blond hair moved to the wind that we generated; some would stick to his sweaty forehead and many others continued to dance around his head. That night was shining.

"NO!" I heard her roar. "Stop! You don't understand!"

I had made her angry.

The last ball of energy she threw at me was right at the very moment when something hit my body. Had I been in another situation, I would have known it was an alarm signal; I would not have forced my power to make a breakthrough in the imaginary wall before me, I simply would have understood that, beyond what I saw, my energy had collided with a hazard. Although I could not have imagined what kind of horror I would receive me beyond the edge of the forest...

It was a sensation similar to leaving Hecate's shelter, although that was even harder. The ground changed and my feet were sinking in the sand with every step. I felt the blows of an energy that, at that moment, believed they belonged to Hecate. I had to show her that I wouldn't be able to hide nothing more! And by the time the water wetted my feet, I felt a current of electricity entering my body, burning inside. It was what had made that shot in me, but this time, through all my being. I was unable to slow down my impetus to find out what Hecate was hiding and now I was lost. Once it reached my waist, I couldn't bear the pain anymore. It was so intense that it made me lose reality.

A flurry of images shattered my mind into thousands of pieces; my arms failed and I could not hold Bruce; I opened my eyes, but water prevented me from seeing beyond what was happening in my head.

Some arms. A long blond mane...

I sank hopelessly, I could do nothing. The water had burned my body, convicting me to the terrible pain I thought I had escaped. When I had drowned in the images that were formed deep in my mind, a strong hand attracted me towards itself. It was not a real hand, if not a cluster of energy that surrounded me completely and took me out of the terrible hole that I had gotten into. I broke the surface of the water with my inert body, but I no longer saw stars in the firmament. I knew

I was safe despite having the feeling of being watched by big eyes, they were too far away to have caught me.

An instant before my back hit on the ground, dry and safe, I imagined his big eyes fixed on mine. The same eyes with which I had already meet so long ago; a creature that had taken everything from me... I saw Hecate, who was screaming at me, but I wasn't able to hear her. The memory I had lost in my mind, from the moment they locked us in the other world, had left me between a state of well-being and terror. Paralyzed, the last light coming out of the crosier that was holding that human, was hitting me squarely again in the body. We would be the bright-eyed creature's food.

Hecate shouted...

I knew that the memory came to the most painful moment, the moment I had never forgotten. When her beautiful blue eyes and her long blond mane faded away forever.

A knot was formed inside me. The pain that had produced in me the exposure to the water was already fading away, eclipsed by a feeling that damaged more than any physical pain; a farewell that not even was able to occur... Because the beast that stalked us at the bottom of the great abyss did not allow it to us. The same beast that I had murdered to get out and go back to our home... A home where there was only death.

I had my mind somewhere else. I couldn't say where exactly: if in the big house where my father would probably be dead, or deep in the ocean, where my mother had done it.

I lost track of time and space. I sprang to my feet and tried to flee from there, from that place that had brought me so much pain. Hecate passed her arms around my waist, to prevent me from walking well. We gave several missteps in the sand that was less cold. And when I could not bear the anguish that caused the sway of the water in my ears, the great knot was transformed into sound and burst from my throat to the sky. It was a devastating howl. Everything I had endured since our arrival was spurting out of my body. All the energy that had been rotting within me, created by so many deaths in our community, was finally coming out. In the shouting I eliminated the pain caused by my mother's death, by Aingeru's; also, the overwhelming feeling of not knowing if the only creature near me was still alive. The scream helped me leave all those feelings behind.

I collapsed on the ground. Hecate released me. I looked around, wanting to find Bruce safe and sound. He was beside her with his face drenched and his eyes reddened by the water. He seemed very tired; he was hungry and all those human needs that I did not understand, nor was I able to satisfy. What's more, I wasn't even able to keep him safe anymore. The lassitude that I saw on Bruce's face joined the big knot that was forming on my chest. Recovering a memory like that wasn't proving easy. It was so strange to know that there was something in the world that had defeated us and we had done everything we could to forget... ah, that infamous crosier that banished us to the other world. I had to do everything possible to try to see more of that part of our existence, no matter how painful that was for me; I had to see more of that red prison, which faded away into my mind.

"Now I see it," I mumbled. "Now I see it..."

I threw myself in the sand, trying to immerse myself in the memory... All my family defeated, doomed to spend eternity in that prison. That image would not be erased again: the face of the only human who had confronted us, decomposed by fear and the ray of light that came out of the crosier that he was hoisting, with the sole purpose of sinking us forever at the bottom of the ocean.

Was it satisfaction what I observed in Hecate's face? Damn smiling demon. Everything that had happened was part of her plan of getting me into the water. For what? Did she want to teach me all that she had learned over so many years with humanity in a single instant? No. She didn't want us to get to the sea. She smiled for something else...

We decided to stay on the beach so Bob and Bruce could catch something to eat. Bob was the one who mastered it, but Bruce had endeavored to learn. I remained sitting under the shade of some palm trees. I had the full armor after my accident in the water. I thought that the less close of me I saw the sea, the safer I would be. Hecate, however, did not seem to worry about the water, or whatever was inside of it, she was simply engaged in drawing pictures in the sand with her feet.

"Are you going to burn the whole beach?" I asked her so that she would feel bad about the energy she was giving off.

She stopped immediately.

"What's the matter? Did the bath made you sick?"

I stood up like a spring and took two big strides towards her. So close to the water I had to concentrate, to hit her. Hecate pushed me, as If she really thought I was going to fall. Her corrosive energy burned for a few moments my armor, which quickly regenerated. Bruce and Bob were far away, but I could hear their shouting.

I did not recognize the drawing that Hecate had made in the sand. I was very angry with her for letting me fall into the water and for playing with us in such a twisted way. Anyway, what did I expect? If she hated everything I represented. At that moment I felt the fatigue falling on my back, like a great rock.

"It wasn't my fault that you decided to come alone," I said, not feeling like wanting to give her a good beating. "Nor is it that you have become a demon."

She seemed confused; but she soon turned into laughter. The humans were approaching as fast as the waves allowed them, they really feared that Hecate and I would fight. I was hoping they wouldn't believe they could stop it.

"Blame me, if so you wish!" She spat.

"If you didn't behave like a damn human we wouldn't have these problems," I hissed. My comparison did not seem to hurt her, as after all, she was already a strange mixture of us all. I made a sign to Bruce so they would stop playing in the water and come to join us. "That will certainly be a problem," I said, pointing to Hecate's feet.

She took her hair with both hands and watched them exaggeratingly. I had the gift of growing hatred within me.

"Mmmm," she mumbled. She grabbed the two tufts of blond hair that she had between her fingers and approached them to her chin. "And what do you suggest we do? I can't help to burn the things that I step on after..."

Bob sat beside us, trying not to look straight at me. He still seemed quite affected by the bloody episode we had shared. Bruce wanted to dry his clothes, I saw him picking up pieces of twigs to make a small bonfire. As he walked from one side to the other, they were falling.

"Oh, please!" I cried out, exasperated at his inability to ignite the bonfire. I threw a small amount of energy and the fire sputtered. "That's real fire" I told Hecate. "Not that ridiculous green thing."

"Bah. What do you know about fire?" She answered me, crossing her arms over her chest.

I was about to answer her when Bob stepped in.

"You can make them disappear," we both looked at him, as if he had never stood there.

"Of course! That's little magic," jabbered Bruce, with a piece of food in his mouth. "You just have to step where Hecate steps..." He added, looking at me. I don't know what it was that reflected my face because he ended up deviated the gaze. "Or you can give her your boots."

"No!" I cried out, vehemently. "I won't give it to anyone! And least of all to you!"

I watched the black tissue diluting to my will, dripping upward until it freed my ankles. And suddenly, life flowing from me to the ground, forming small plants that entangled in my fingers. If I wanted to keep moving, I'd have to break them. I dropped an exasperated sigh and headed for the absurd drawing of Hecate. I passed one foot above it and it happened what we expected. The plants hid the trace of corrosion.

"Well," Hecate accepted. "Finish eating and we'll leave here. Now we know what to find."

"Stop laughing!" I snapped at her. "At least, I try to do something and not like you, that only hinder our way."

"That I...!"

"Enough!" Bob exploded. "Hecate has lost control and she apologizes for it."

I devoted a hatred-laden look to her, who folded her arms and never spoke to us any more, until the next incident. She was really unbearable. As for Bob, I looked at him on that occasion, as if it was the first time. His body was that of a warrior and his face of soft features contrasted with the scar on his cheek. That gave him an air of danger that would surely have helped him intimidate someone, on more than one occasion. To see that strange couple was curious to me, at the same that it was tiresome. I was wishing for the moment when we had to split, almost as much as finding the weapon.

The humans and I talked for hours about what was the best way to find the great crosier of my memories. It was beginning to impress me the natural way in which we talked; I no longer felt that pressure and disgust, knowing that I was so close to a living human, different from Bruce. My inside had changed, thanks to the first glimpse of some eyes filled with light; human eyes. Bruce noticed that I was watching him, he smiled at me and continued giving ideas. The conversation became exclusive of them. I tried to focus, but the great gleam of that last memory of this world, eclipsed me completely...

...A large bluish crosier, crowned by a large oval stone, as clear and shiny as a cloud-covered sky; it was surrounded by two branches, which were darkening until they looked like a pair of sharp fingernails. And the human who carried it... what was he like? Did he have anything else? I had to be able to freeze the memory and try to set everything else aside and be able to see his face.

We had been walking for hours when I became aware of the silence around us. Something had made Bruce and Bob stop talking about our goal. I felt nothing around us that was what worried me most.

"Hecate," I whispered. She was walking in front of me, as we had decided, to avoid leaving traces, at a distance to which even a human would have listened to me. "Hecate," I insisted. Bob took his hand to his waist, where he kept the metal rod, with which he had defeated those Hunters in the forest. "Demon!"

"What?" She demanded vehemently, stopping the march. "What is your wish, O great princess?"

I grunted, but it wasn't time for arguing. Something was surrounding us and it wasn't a Hunter. Even humans felt that the environment was getting rarified at times.

"Is your instinct atrophied?" I said, about to lose my patience. The plants grew around my feet, tangled up to my knees. "Enough! I'm sick of you! I will search the crosier alone and I will recover the community." I made my armor seal the energy. I knew Bruce would follow me, so I didn't even look back. I walked swiftly forward, still with the feeling of being observed by something; something I wasn't able to feel. I wanted to get away as much as I could from the sea, which blocked my abilities. Before leaving them behind, I wanted to add: "Oh, and after I cut off his head, I'll nail him to the door of your dominions."

Hecate frowned, but said nothing when she saw us leave.

Bruce had done nothing but to express his restlessness, for having dispensed with them. It became clear that the other human delighted him, if he could still be called that. It did not surprise me at all that he missed the company of an equal, to speak or simply to know that it was running, in a way, the same thing through his veins. I coped as I could with the increasingly less tolerable, Bruce's complaints, only by thinking that I would find the crosier and I would manage to save my entire community. However, the memory of our defeat was distorted every time I tried to know who was the human who had condemned us all.

In the midst of my anger, I felt a cold hand near mine. I made full stop. I couldn't believe Bruce had touched me and I wouldn't have set aside. I turned slowly, to look him in the eye; those eyes that had caused so much damage to us all. He seemed so small...

"I'm sorry I couldn't do anything when..." his voice broke before he finished talking.

"What are you talking about?" We were in the middle of the forest and until just a few seconds ago, it invaded me the insecurity of not having hundred per cent of my energy; however, his concern took away mine.

The rays of sunshine produced reflections in his dark eyes; nothing like ours. He possessed a vitality that our power didn't reach. Bruce had something we wanted and it was his purity. I had to make sure that it remained intact.

"I couldn't get you out of the water," he completed, crestfallen. "I thought it was again like when your leg..."

"It's not your fault!" I hastened to stop him. Humans, it seems, have the need to blame themselves or someone else. They are not able to simply accept that there are things that happen and cannot be avoided. In that case, however, there was one culprit. "Come on," I urged him, taking my hand away from his. "We have long way to go."

"But if you don't know where to go." He replied to me. "You've only seen what we have to find. Besides," he added, "I know you think it's nonsense, but I don't think we'll find anything."

"And why not?" I asked him, stopping the march. "Why don't you think we can find anything?"

He sat on a log, we had been walking for hours and he was exhausted.

"Because there are already two people in the world who have found it," he leaned back, closed his eyes and added, "and I don't want to be around them, even to take away something that will help us..."

A sigh came out of the depths of my being; a sigh that resembled more an exorbitant yell. Something broke inside me. I had not stopped to think about the fear that Bruce felt, due to all that was happening, I had not believed that he was so afflicted.

"Well!"

"Oh, tell me that it isn't...!"

Hecate and Bob appeared, out of nowhere. They acted as if we had not argued: she sat next to Bruce, with her legs stretched and Bob supported the weight of his body against a nearby trunk.

"Here," Bruce," he said, holding out a handful of roots. "I grabbed them near here."

I fixed my eyes on Bruce, I couldn't believe I would have behaved that way with him and above all, what was most incredible to me was how much it affected me. The fact that it produced so much fear in him to confront Bayron and his brother... so much as not to share with any of us that possibility to begin with, made me think that perhaps, none of that would be happening, if it was not for me; If I hadn't dragged Bruce into my madness, he wouldn't be afraid. Soon a thought arose like a knife, it turned me away from that worry I felt and let me drowning in another one; one that I could not solve: I could only see that flash of light, destroying everything I loved.

I was not going to allow the traitor of Bayron to get what he was looking for; nor was I going to allow it to Hecate.

For several moments we remained silent; too overwhelmed to articulate a word. After such a long time fleeing from the Hunter who had betrayed us all, how it was possible that it had not passed through my mind, not even for a second, that that was the most possible reason for the existence of these weapons. I sighed. Perhaps that explosion would have unleashed in me all the emotions that I thought buried, and being so close to humans, turned me into a fool; It was clear that they had indeed transformed Hecate in a certain way. I watched her for a moment (I was just trying to run away from my own reproaches), she had been distracted following the flight of a yellow butterfly. She seemed simply happy, as if nothing of what was happening in my world touched her own. Was she so sure she could survive alone? And as if she had heard what I was thinking, she devoted a deep look to me. I was determined to stop being her entertainment. She was fire and I was the air that would make her burn.

We walked till it started to dusk. We would have to find a place for both humans to sleep and we could think quietly, what our next move should be. I thought it was clear that I didn't want to continue the trip with them, but apparently they didn't care. And Bruce had left me too confused to protest; so, again, my feet were barefoot, stepping on the scorched tracks that Hecate left on the floor.

It must have been very hard not to be able to touch anything that was in nature. If the world in which we both lived was as important to her as the one in which only she and Bob fit, then she would be right. Not being able to feel the energy that the trees and animals gave me, for me it would have been a terrible end; she seemed at ease. To go closing the march allowed me to look at all her expressions. I was about to believe that for her nothing that surrounded her was truly important, until I saw a deep sadness at the bottom of her light blue eyes. It was only a brief moment, but there it was. In that brief lapse of time, I could see that the path she had chosen was too hard. Surely from that comes her horrible taste for games.

"What is that?" Bruce's question made me go back to the world we were in now.

"It's a subway entrance," said Hecate and Bob in unison.

They looked at each other and smiled tenderly.

A few steps ahead, there was a sort of underground road. It was covered in the brush. It was incredible to me that there were still human constructions, throughout the world. I hoped that nature itself would take care of destroying it completely. The trees around it, gave it shade during the day, so it would be almost invisible, even when it was daytime... I crouched the head, completely ignoring Hecate's corrosive steps, there were no traces of any kind. It was too strange that there would have been no animals on our tour. At first, I thought it was Hecate, but now that she was at my side and her energy was at rest, that idea did not seem to be the most viable. I looked for her with my eyes and she was worried too. Damn. The humans, on the other hand, were excited: "We will be able to sleep under cover". "How good! We won't be cold tonight". As if going inside was a good idea...

Anyway, I had to go in first, because I wasn't going to let Bruce face the vision of some murdered human. Hecate came in last place. To tell the truth, there was nothing suspicious and it would help us travel in a more discreet way. I lifted the palm of my hand and lit a little green energy, to lower the tension between Hecate and me. She laughed at the color of what lit the way. During that moment, I thought we could get to something more than to tolerate each other.

The drop of light was opening through the darkness, in front of Bruce and Bob; Hecate walked beside me, entangling her arms between mine. A part of me was sure that her intention was to make me fall.

"You know?" She said, in such a loud whisper. "I'd like to finish him too," I didn't answer her. I didn't want to talk in that tunnel, where I felt my energy was crushed against me. "We could spend the night here," what was she saying? Why did she behave so strangely?

Bruce and Bob turned to look at us, the energy ball fluctuated and it was when I understood what Hecate was aiming for: she wanted the humans that were surrounding us, to know that we were not as they believed. What had led her to that, had been not being able to see them? I didn't see them either. I only perceived shadows that slipped everywhere. Would it be some other exiled who had given the gift of energy to a group of the sub-race?

"Yes," I said, with a tense voice. "We will wait for Bruce and Bob to rest and we will continue in the morning," Hecate encouraged me with the look to continue. I hesitated for a moment, but I decided to follow the game, "we'll find a way to end them. I'm sure."

"What?" Bruce burst. "How can you say that now, if...?"

"Are you starting a quarrel now?" Hecate stopped him.

It was clear that Bruce and Bob had not seen the humans around us in the shadows. I did not want that the instinct that had made me kill so many, would gush inside me, forcing me to kill everyone; I had to get control of myself again, for Bruce. But that situation seemed to be different from the one I had lived, just before I met Hecate.

Bruce sat on the platform we had in front of us, he fiddled with his legs as the ball of light sizzled around him. He thought it was my thing, that I did it to cheer him up and he wasn't so sulky; he smiled at me from the gloom, when two black hands slid down his face and dragged him into the darkness.

"BRUCE!"

My body dived, without even thinking about it for a moment, in the heavy blackness surrounding the subway tracks. Hecate and Bob followed me few steps away. I wondered if the creature that had Bruce would be some kind of hybrid like Bob was, but it didn't seem to be like that, for as much as I struggled, it was impossible for me to spot him in the dark. I heard Bruce screaming a few meters beyond, in the depths. Hecate did what she could to get my attention, but at that moment, in which I believed that the life of my human was in danger,

I was not able to pay attention to anything that was not the trace I had to follow. I was no longer ready to contain my cravings to rip off the heads of all humans that I might find from now on; nor would I continue with any other game of which Hecate would like to make me a participant, because, having snitched on the position of those around us, none of that would be happening.

The armor buzzed in my ears, it was so full of energy that it was very likely to end up exploding in any way. The fear of losing Bruce, had made me lose control, almost entirely.

"Bruce!" I cried out to the shadows.

And all of a sudden I saw myself in a little room illuminated by a white, flickering light. Whoever took Bruce had just left. There was only one door by which I wanted us to go out. I approached Bruce, who was on the floor, with a lost gaze.

"Bruce." I didn't receive an answer. I was in a state of shock. "Hey!"

"They had drugged him," said Hecate. "It's a menace. Apparently, they think we're human. They're so stupid they haven't even stopped to think we had a floating ball that gave off light."

"What are you talking about?"

"Look," she said to me, removing from Bruce's chest a paper with the drawing of a «Y» in black. "I don't know what this means," she crumpled the paper and burned it between her tattooed fingers. "Come on!" she pushed me. "Remove from him whatever they had injected him and let's go find the person responsible for this."

She seemed so calm; distant to the state I was in. That is how I should look: a tempered energy, and a serene face, because truth be told, there was only one thing that could get in my way.

I sighed. I closed my eyes and probed Bruce, looking for the substance that paralyzed his body and found that he had a small wound by which it had probably entered. His heart was beating so slowly... Again, the fear of losing him returned to me; the fear of never seeing that light again. It was not very difficult to know where the problem was, I withdrew the chain that held him prisoner and I waited until he regained full control of his body.

"Let's go ahead," Hecate announced. "Angelyne will take you and the four of us will be protected by a strong field of energy, until we find who has done this to you."

"It was horrible," whispered Bruce in my ear, after the march began. "His arms were warm, almost as much as yours," he continued to say. It seemed incredible to me, that those beings would not have realized what kind of creatures they had offended; "He had a lot of strength," he continued, as we got more and more into the depths.

If something unexpected happened, I would simply have to jump, just as I had done in the Hunters' den. I didn't understand why I was so worried; surely it would be for not knowing what we were facing. Running and running after a shadow that would surely have the energy of a being like us was not something that would allow me to be calm.

"Keep talking to me," I made a pause before I pronounced his name, "Bruce."

Further on, there was a big hole, which we had to jump to move forward. That's what confirmed my suspicions, it definitely could not be a mere human.

"Do you think it's going to be someone like Bob?" He asked me. He didn't care that Hecate or Bob himself could hear him. "I remember how I felt when I you gave part of your energy to me," his voice acquired a nostalgic tone, as if he wondered that if he hadn't gone with me that night, he would have ended up dead among the walls of the great mansion.

"Do not be afraid," I said, when his shivering was evident. "I'll protect you."

Bruce wouldn't be able to see my expression in that darkness. If I had believed, only five minutes ago, that I was going to be hunting a human and protecting another... It was so ironic. I released a laughter, which resonated forcefully and was lost with the echo.

"What's so funny, princess?" Told me Hecate. She was also worried about our opponent.

"Nothing."

I accelerated the step and took the great leap that separated us from another lit room, in which a dark silhouette was visible.

"I think it was a woman," whispered Bruce, after a great sigh. "I think whoever dragged me into the room was a woman."

The minute we went through the room, I could see her. Either because of Bruce's words or because I was at a distance where no kind of energy could hide her. Hecate stood beside me, with the same dismayed expression that was in my face. She hid Bob behind her back. It was as if she was waiting for the female human who was in front of us, to act first.

She had brown hair and very long, too long for her little body; though her muscles were strong and she did not remind me at all of any of the humans I had eliminated so far. It was leaning against the frame of a door, with a carefree attitude. She didn't even care that we were there. That infuriated me so much that, without releasing Bruce, I threw a projectile of energy, which hit the target. I didn't want to kill her. That was the only reason why seconds later, when the smoke had already dissipated, she looked at us with eyes wide opened; now she knew who she was dealing with.

"Well!" She squealed, as if by hearing her own voice, she were to feel less unprotected. "I set a trap for thieves," confidence was gradually returning to her words. "And what a surprise! Some assassins have fallen."

The strange affection that Hecate had developed towards humans prevented her from speaking; and what prevented me was the great contempt I felt for them.

"What do you know!" Bruce exploded, surprising us all.

"Human..." The girl stammered. That vision had produced more horror in her than the blow of my energy. "What...?" She shook her head. "They are not going to like this at all. We will see if with that energy so poor," she added, setting herself at the ready for a run, "you managed to finish us off."

She smiled. And the last thing I saw, before she vanished into darkness, was her eyes; some eyes that I had seen before, in another place... eyes of the creature that had snatched it all away from me. The eyes of that female human and those of the traitor were the same. A pair of yellow eyes.

Part 2:

«An Appointment in the Other World, that World in Which They Only Talk about Death»

Chapter 10

«Hecate's Descendants»

We ran after her for several hours, believing she would soon get tired. Even Bob had to sleep and eat. The underground roads were deserted and overpopulated with insects and rodents. Where that elusive female human would be driving us? I listened to the sound of Bruce's agitated breathing, mingling with the puddles that we stepped on as we got deep, at the bottom of that black hole. I wondered how frightened the young man should feel, for he was the only one who saw absolutely nothing.

We got to a pretty well-lit platform. That place... I saw some strings arranged from end to end of the platform. I was going to jump on the tracks when I heard Hecate screaming.

"Stop, Stop!"

I fully stopped, causing her to almost collide with me. I looked at her begging for forgiveness, she gave me back a look full of rage. She let Bob go and straightened her hair with both hands. I did the same thing with Bruce, who walked away from me, ignoring the danger he was in, being the only mortal in the group.

"What's the matter?" I asked her. "We were about to catch her."

"Ha!" She spat. "She has escaped. We've been running blind for over four hours. And is not that she is tired," she added, rolling her eyes, "I don't want to spend my life chasing a human."

We argued loud for a while, even Bob participated in the exalted talk with enthusiasm. It was as if he had suddenly been reactivated and able to give arguments that contradicted his mistress. Our words rose in the air loud, surrounded by my energy and Hecate's, everything around us was strange, until we heard the sound of an engine behind our back. We all turned around at the same time, ready to defend ourselves, fearing it was something we couldn't control, when we saw Bruce in a wagon, smiling.

"Hey! I 've managed to make it work," he leaned on one of the doors and he made a sign with his hand to us, so we would get close.

The unbelief that had arisen within me must have kept me anchored, while the blond demon jumped beside me.

"Terrific!" Hecate cried out. "It had been so many years since I did not travel by Subway...!"

She rushed inside the wagon, colliding against poor Bruce. She ran across the cabin, leaving black footprints on her way and jumping. I did not know if what was drawn in her face was a real expression of happiness.

"Whatever!" Sighed Bob, getting in with heaviness.

Bruce got up with a smile on his face. He held one of his shoulders with his hand, due to the blow that Hecate had given him.

"Let's go!" He stretched out a hand towards me. That human thingy didn't produce the slightest confidence in me.

I sighed. I figured that my face would look just like I saw Bob's. I took the hand of the human, who made the gesture of pulling hard of me. To make him feel better, I gave myself a little impulse and fell on the ground in the same way that I would have fallen if he had been stronger than myself.

The door was jammed, so we decided to leave it open. Bob was sprawled on the ground, he nodded at us, as he took out of one of his pockets something to eat and threw it at Bruce.

When they had finished eating, Bruce approached the place where the car's controls were. I saw him move between all the buttons and a central lever, which, I assumed, would be the brake and the accelerator. It was growing inside me a desire to be the one to drive that contraption; besides, it was clear that Bruce had no idea how to do it.

At the very moment that I was going to open my mouth, Bruce managed to get it started. Hecate gave a shriek of excitement. I felt that we began to move at a good speed, it seemed that we all enjoyed the trip, even Bruce, who was the only one who was not able to maintain the balance the same way we did.

Some lights passed quickly on both sides, I was surprised that there was electricity. Perhaps, what we would find later was the responsible. Would it be a human colony? I wondered. I observed Hecate and Bob, who had sat together quietly, enjoying the memories that that journey by subway brought them. I dwelt at the details of the artifact, rusting everywhere and traces of what one day was red paint; If none of that was relevant, that place was nice. I saw the tunnel, which seemed to have no end, dimly lit by the headlights, Bruce's head was almost invisible in the prevailing darkness of the cockpit.

"This is fun," he said, breaking the silence.

I was bored, having had something to discharge my attention, we would have had no inconvenience. I approached swiftly to the lever, which Bruce held with his hands.

"Let me do it," I tried to turn him away, but I didn't want to hurt him, "you don't know."

"No!" He shouted. "I'm driving it," he did put all his effort into turning me away.

I laughed to make him nervous and he would loosen up, without having to do anything to him, but he had determined not to disengage voluntarily. We moved the lever up and down, for a moment I thought it would break, but nothing else happened, apart from abrupt braking and accelerating. I heard Hecate and Bob complain further back; but what I heard later (what Bruce and I heard), it did make the trip fun: the lever was not ready to withstand so much pressure and ended up breaking. Bruce remained with it in his hand, while the wagon was rushing to the depths hopelessly.

"Okay," he gave in, with the fear drawn in his eyes. "You do it," he added, giving me the piece of the lever.

"Oh, no, no, no!" I rejected, giving it back to him. "You were right, I have to leave you alone."

"Great, mumbled Hecate. "Now the train is going to crash. You must be happy, aren't you? Now we can never ride the subway again."

To scare Bruce a little and to get even because he didn't want to give me the lever before the incident, I activated the whole armor, even covering my head.

"Uh! That's not fair," he squealed, curling up into a ball on the ground.

"All right," I whispered. I couldn't bear to see him so frightened, even though it was all a little joke. "Come here."

I knelt next to Bruce and covered both with my energy, just the instant the train hit something and started spinning in the air. I kept my eyes open and saw that Hecate held Bob by the hand; for them there was no gravity for that moment. Finally, we crashed with violence. When the dust was dissipated, I raised my energy to let Bruce move, who seemed confused and dizzy. By the way his face looked, I knew right away what he was going to do.

"How gross!" Mumbled Hecate, leaving quickly.

I waited for Bruce to put back together.

"Are you ok?"

"Yes," he mumbled, his face was very white. "But I'm not feeling too well."

"Let's go!" I encouraged him. "Get in my arms."

Smiling, he walked with heaviness to where I was. I raised him effortlessly, and before he was completely asleep, he allowed himself the luxury of whispering in my ear something that kept me worried, even after I saw him awake again:

"If I were like you, you wouldn't have to worry so much about me."

I tried to wake him up to repeat, if he had courage, what he had just said, but it was in vain. As I waited for my thoughts to be put in order, I remembered the strange eyes that we were chasing. What would that mean? Perhaps, I seem to have imagined such a color in the gaze of Bayron, in all our encounters, but that girl... Oh, no, I never imagined that.

I heard a rasping noise that got me out of my absorption. It came from outside the fallen wagon. It had been totally wrecked. Thanks to my field of energy, we had not felt any of the blows when turning in the air. I fell all the way down to the door, fed up about everything that was happening around us. More and more I liked less the idea of having to find a crosier that I vaguely remembered, in order to save the community.

"We have new little friends," I heard a voice say. A voice I didn't recognize.

Without showing my astonishment, I looked up to the new group of humans in front of us. Among them was the girl after which we ran; she was leaning against a dirty wall, but she didn't seem to mind that detail. After all, I said to myself, that was where they lived. I looked around and I could only see a disturbingly thick darkness, surely there would be more like them hidden. I didn't like the fact that they were able to hide from us.

In the center of the group, who gave off the greatest amount of energy was a tall and very swarthy woman, her hair caught my attention a lot of. They all wore light clothes (except for the first girl we had seen) and very uncomfortable to respond to a melee attack. The woman's shoes were sharp and made her look taller than she was. I noticed the appearance of the other three men who accompanied them: they were all strong and fibrous, but the color of their skin was similar to mine. They were waiting for our reaction, they were suspicious; and even if they could hide from us, they couldn't hide that they were afraid. The last detail that stuck to my chest like a stake, was to see that they all had bright, amber eyes.

I felt that Bruce was starting to wake up, I turned him gently and left him on the floor beside me. He still felt dizzy and could barely stand upright. His body temperature had risen too much in a few moments, and the movement of his chest as he breathed, little by little was transformed into large puffs, which did not match the expected result. However, at that time I did not understand anything about the human body and I let it pass.

"Hello," I said, passing an arm through Bruce's waist.

That not only baffled the people we had before us, but it also did to Hecate and Bob. The humans stared at the woman with the extravagant hair; that confirmed to me that she was their leader.

"Come on, Monique," whispered one of them, believing that we could not hear him. "Tell her something."

Monique was staring at us. Her yellow eyes flickered hard. I wondered what kind of energy that was. The black trousers that covered her legs, shrank when she tensed the muscles; I could see that, despite not having a threatening appearance —as the first girl we had encountered—her body was ready for a fight. She undid her jacket, revealing the sword that was tied to her belt and a shirt of an unpolluted white. I found it curious that all those creatures were dressed in the same way.

"Monique!" Repeated the same human.

She sighed.

"I don't know what to say!" She complained. "I never thought I'd meet any of them face to face." She recognized, raising her shoulders as an apology.

The three humans rolled their eyes. They seemed as confusing as we were. It was clear that they knew we were not going to kill them without a word; what was not so clear, was what we were doing down there. I don't know how long we would have spent looking at each other, waiting for someone to give a first step, had it not been for Bruce, who started screaming because of the pain.

"Bruce!"

He threw himself on the floor, holding his wounded hand. I knelt beside him, fearing the worst. At that instant, the certainty of his mortality struck me and made me believe that his end had come. I forgot that he was a fragile person and it had been too long without us paying attention to his needs.

"Oh, shit!" Cried out one of the men. "They carry a human!"

"I told you it was true!" the girl who had kidnapped him burst. She walked towards the man who had spoken with determination and delivered him a punch in the face that knocked him to the ground. "Unbeliever. Every day I dislike you more."

"Enough!" Monique made them shut up with just one word. They feared her. "Aymerick, François! Bring something for the kid."

She looked at me, as if a certainty in her mind had suddenly become something that was not true.

"We have always known that you were not like humans thought you were," those words and their smiles made me look at Hecate, who was more concerned with keeping Bob away from all that than listening to humans. "Julien and Eugène can help him down here."

I noticed then that those two humans, were identical. They had the same tone of brown hair and the same features.

"Here you have a bandage to disinfect," Aymerick threw a small package into Julien's arms, who hurried to clean the wound that was oozing pus and showing a rather reddened appearance.

There were no visible changes in him, which worried me.

"What animal has left such a bite? Aren't you guys careful?" She snapped at us.

"Shut up!" Monique silenced her. "They didn't have to know."

"Oh, you're always defending them!" Burst Aymerick. It seemed that she did not like us.

The twins offered to carry Bruce, to which I said no; I would be the one to take care of him. Now that they had saved the life of the human, we would be back again in the beginning.

"You say you are not human," Hecate began, separating from Bob. If she did not intervene, she would end up bursting, "then what are you?"

I looked at them all. There was a big black opening on the wall that was at their backs, for which they would certainly have arrived. Aymerick had sat on the floor turning her back on us, to show everyone that she wasn't the slightest excited about this meeting; François did the same thing trying to look away from Bob, who did not seem to feel uncomfortable by the admiration that he was receiving; the twins were behind Monique, who looked at Hecate, with an improper expectation of the moment in which we were all in.

"We are the descendants of the Atlantes," I could not overlook the longing tone with which she uttered that word. "The gods who were confined to the depths of the ocean" a memory of murky waters, shook my mind.

I shook Bruce more strongly than I should, to feel that he had not left the subway; he slightly grumbled. One of the bulbs on the ceiling flickered and we stayed a few moments in shadows. When the light came back, I observed that Monique's eyes had been moistened. The appearance of her face was fragile, which contrasted with her firm and tense body, hidden under a layer of cloth.

"Ah..." sighed Aymerick. "We should go back, your sister must be worried," she went to the opening, and before she jumped, she addressed to us a sidelong look. Half her face vanished in the shadows. "And more she is going to be."

François followed her without a word.

I heard their footsteps moving away in the blackness.

"I always knew there was more strength in her muscles than in her faith," mumbled one of the twins, adopting a more carefree attitude.

"Personally," Monique began, approaching the door; "I never thought I would see any of you so close and less in these circumstances," she pointed out. "But, it is a great honor for me to have you before me," she took the right palm of her hand to her chest and bowed slightly, leaving the other arm behind her, as a sign of respect for us.

Hecate looked at me. She did not seem to be at ease with the change that was taking our mission. What I was worried about was the way they had to refer to themselves...

"... The descendants of the banished to..."

"... The depths!" Eugène stopped me.

He was immediately reprimanded by his twin brother for interrupting me. I managed to capture the vital difference between the two; it was so slight that I would not even have noticed it had I not observed that argument: it was a point in the energy they gave off; a very small stain on Julien's energy, blue color. That's what helped me distinguish them at the rest of our moments with them.

"Our..." I hesitated. It was a very shocking situation for me. I had Bruce fainted in the arms, Hecate and Bob at my side, without saying a word, and a group of humans who claimed to be our descendants.

I sighed.

I remembered, thanks to my fatal incursion in the water, that we had been banished by a human who used a crosier, to achieve such a feat. But what I would never have imagined was that a group of humans would claim themselves as our heirs. Although the truth was that as I watched them, that idea didn't seem so crazy. That speed, that way of making shine their inner power... It was all too surreal.

Monique cleared her throat and I returned to the present where we were.

"Forgive me," she began to say, with her hands clasped. "I know that for you, time does not mean the same as for us... so," it was as if she had forgotten to speak completely, "if you don't mind, would you be so kind as to answer a little faster?" I frowned, Hecate had lifted the eyebrows. "Just a little bit!"

"How about you come with us?" Julien hastened to intervene. "That poor boy is in the bones and he could bath and have some clean clothes..." He observed Hecate and his eyes widely opened. "We can share with you what you need."

Whatever you need! If they claimed to be our descendants, they would have a more concrete idea of what led us to that red prison. On the other hand... if what they wanted was to deceive us to kill everyone with that same contraption, we should be very attentive.

"Very well!" I agreed. "We'll go with you," Hecate didn't even move a muscle when she heard me talk. I didn't know what she was trying to do, but I didn't even want to imagine it. "You're very kind," I added gently.

They seemed happy with my change of attitude. It was as if they were waiting, for a long time, for similar words. I wondered what kind of creatures we would encounter after we reached the end of that dark tunnel, by which we get in now. I felt that my eyes shone when we plunged into that corridor in gloom.

We arrived at a circular chamber, decorated with strange engravings on the walls, lit only with torches. There lay before us another long passage, little brighter than the one we had just crossed. I watched the drawings, they were circles that collided in the center and got separated again, surrounded by what seemed to be flames; there was also a figure that reminded me slightly of someone I already knew. Bob burst into laughter as he saw the image of the creature. The humans were confused, but they decided to continue walking. The next stay was of excessive proportions, which made me think it was a gigantic lair under the ground.

"Now, I will introduce you to my sister Anaëlle," Monique's smile was very white, I couldn't help but match it with the color of her skin. I couldn't get used to seeing so many types of humans. "She has also been waiting you for a long time."

We crossed the room's threshold; its roof was so high that we could have been in any of our forms. I was surprised that they had managed to make that refuge dug in stone. I looked at Bruce, to see if he was observing the same thing I did, but what I saw alarmed me: his face had acquired a bluish tone that gave it more of a corpse appearance, than of being something alive.

"How long has he not eaten properly?"

Eat? I didn't have the slightest idea. I saw it with Bob, believing it would be enough. After all, what was it to eat for me?

Monique took it delicately from my arms that in the face of concern, did not even try to hold him back. I saw her take him away, but I never stopped feeling him at any time. I didn't know what the humans were doing to him, but it seemed to be paying off, because I immediately noticed that Bruce's energy was stabilizing.

I lowered my guard and refocused on the others. The figure that had amused Bob so much was sculpted in the rock of the hall, right in the center, focusing his blessing on the members of the great black table that stood out in the room. The face of black eyes, which were once blue; a quiet smile, instead of that mocking gesture I knew so well: a work that only human love was capable of generating.

"It can't be..." I jabbered.

"What's the matter?" Inquired Hecate. "Oh!" She cried out as she saw her own face. "This is me!"

She took a turn on herself and clasped both hands in front of her chest. Her long blond hair flew like an endless waterfall. Most of the humans got petrified to see her, because in her they had recognized the idol they had been worshipping for so long.

"I didn't think it was true when we felt your energy so close," said a woman, dressed in the same outfit as Monique and the twins. She had blond and smooth hair and the same eyes that disturb me so much. She had leaned against the black table which, contrasted with the fabric of her clothes, shone strongly. "So many years..."

All humans took their right hand to the chest, while leaning on one knee. Hecate came back to my side and took me by one arm. She did not seem to be enjoying at all the homage.

"Anaëlle," Monique began to say, eagerly, "they are..." She stopped immediately, realizing that she didn't know our names. "How are we to address you?"

"Don't you remember what her name is?" I asked, pointing at Hecate and taking her off myself.

"There are many stories about her name," Anaëlle was not afraid of us, like everyone else. She walked slowly towards us. "Many stories of how she saved our ancestors from the ignorance of the human being; of how she gave us a feather of her wings to fly with her until..."

Hecate was very tense. She feared she would lose control at any moment. In the voice of our interlocutor there was a tone of reproach that, if it became a claim, it would plunge Hecate into that deep abyss in which she was trapped.

"Until you left us!" Somebody interrupted.

We turn the face towards the place where Aymerick was. So, that's why she didn't like us. I tried to get between Hecate and her, but the smiling demon gently turned me away. Monique and Anaëlle held each other's hands, it didn't seem to matter to them that someone had said aloud what they were all thinking.

"You must not be more than twenty years old." The words came out of Hecate's lips slowly, with an almost convincing control. "How dare you to demand an explanation to me for something you haven't even lived?"

Aymerick's countenance was darkened, her eyes were drenched and she ran out of the room, knocking down anyone who stood in her way.

Hecate snorted.

The obvious difference between those sisters, caught all my attention. As I understand it, the human siblings keep a regular large resemblance; but those two women, not only did not look alike, but had a completely opposite skin color. I tried not to think of how Ribek and Bruce were alike, without success. I focused on the overwhelming difference between the two, the light that Bruce gave off.

"Please," Monique let go of her sister and approached us. "Apologize her. She hasn't been able to control her temperament."

I felt my armor moving lightly on my body. I had not received any alarm signals, which led me to think that it wanted to be haughty in that situation.

The identical humans had sat at the black table, no other had done so. They were probably the leaders of that community.

"We have so many questions..." a red-haired human addressed to us.

He didn't get to touch me for a few centimeters.

"But," Anaëlle didn't seem very excited about our arrival; at least not as much as the others were. "What I haven't finished understanding is why you have crashed with a subway car, so close to our territory, when it is clear that it was not us who you sought."

"That is not so clear for us," I intervened, taking several steps towards her. "Something has brought us here. Whatever it is. Our paths were destined to unite again," her yellow eyes glimmered lightly, she liked what she was listening to. "And for all that you seem to know about the life that once had Hecate," a murmur rose in the hall, followed by the repetition in whispers of the same name that I had uttered, "that she no longer remembers, I will tell you that the most probable reason why we have found you, might be, because we need your help."

That did surprise them. Even more than admitting that there were things we could forget. I climbed up three steps of the stairs that gave access to the big black table. Monique had her eyes as open as her sister's and the twins had completely dropped their jaw.

I turned the face to observe Hecate's reaction. She gave me back an unfathomable look. Bob was getting tired of eating at one of the tables near the wall, destined to supply the whole room. He was the least interested in how the situation was developing.

"Our..." stammered Anaëlle, the leader, "help."

"That's right," I claimed, taking my hands to my waist.

My armor vibrated insistently. I retired the part that covered my head, leaving my hair out.

"I did not forsake you," Hecate was left behind in the conversation. "It was... an accident. And if you have waited for me to return, through all these years, it is because all of you understand it."

The humans who were in the great hall bowed to her, to show her that they were still with her, despite everything. Then, Anaëlle undid her jacket, just as her sister and said in a powerful voice:

"We'll help you in exchange for something."

"Of what?" I heard myself ask.

"We want you to open the doors to El Dorado for us."

"El Dorado?" I asked surprised.

"Yes," the four claimed in unison.

I lifted an eyebrow, waiting for them to understand that I had not the slightest idea what they were talking about. The silence in the room covered us all, as if it were a raven flying over our heads. I observed the countenance of the four humans before me: In their moistened eyes, one could guess the great desire that was beating within them. Unfortunately, as eager as I was to help them, I still did not know what they wanted.

"In the manuscripts of our ancestors," explained Monique, "they talk about a pure, wonderful place... to which they could only access through their creator."

"Who would become a great serpent," continued to explain Eugène, so feverish that I was surprised, "and would go through the barrier hidden to the eyes of humans to take them to that paradise."

All eyes were fixed on Hecate, even mine. A hidden place on this earth? Nothing that similar have awakened in my memory when I heard its name. She was distracted looking at her sculpted image in the stone, evoking moments that made her smile. After several minutes, we understood that we were not going to receive an answer from her.

"I don't know what El Dorado is," I admitted, afflicted to notice their disappointment. "She escaped before from the prison."

I had before me the four siblings, who exchanged several glances. They tried to understand my words. I could almost see how ideas were placing themselves in their minds; slowly, very slowly, their countenances were changing until they remained with the most confusing expression I had ever seen on the face of a human.

I sighed.

Was I going to have to explain everything?

"Little is what you can help us..." I murmured.

I spent the next few hours explaining to that group of humans what had happened to our species. I told them how we had been locked up at the bottom of the sea and why Hecate had been their savior. I omitted what I knew about the change in her behavior. I didn't want them to believe that, at any moment, she could kill them and eat them all. I also told them that it had been us the ones responsible for the massacre and the end of the world as they knew it.

"Not to be rude," said Julien, interrupting. "But I like things better now."

Everyone agreed with the comment. Those creatures were strange; maybe it was true they weren't human. However, when I looked at them, despite seeing the energy flowing in them in a good way, the mortality that ran through their veins was too obvious. And something else; something that characterizes that race: that feverish effort and that decontrol when it comes to managing emotions. Besides, I had seen what kind of super humans Hecate was able to create.

Monique realized the expression of my face.

"It is not that we rejoice that so many people have died," though I saw no sorrow overshadowing her eyes. "It's just that the world is better now, that they are not here to destroy it."

"Well," said thirdly her sister, "It's dinnertime," she encouraged us to go up to the great table, "even if one of you had moved forward to us," Bob mumbled a barely audible apology.

We were going to share a table with them, with the leaders, so that someone at last —even if I had to be human— would tell me what really happened in that battle. It was then that a spark ignited in my mind a distant memory... An old vision that, by itself, did not seem important: the moment in which Bayron had tried to traverse my body with his spear; the instant I saw the glare of his amber eyes, filled with rage and hatred.

"Wait!" My voice stopped them half way. They looked at me surprised, "why are your eyes of that color?"

"And why are yours blue?" Returned Monique, amused.

"I saw a traitor with that sparkle in his gaze," the words came out pell-mell of my mouth. Perhaps, the one who was about to lose control was me and not Hecate. "The creature who has tried to destroy my race, had eyes like yours!" If I had needed lungs to breathe, I would have fainted.

That statement froze us all for a brief moment, which almost seemed to last for decades. The spirals of smoke that came out of the candles hanging on the walls, fluctuated before my eyes, amusing, as if what I just said was a stupid joke.

The siblings were the first to regain control, either because they did not feel so involved with me or because their life would someday have an end.

"What are you talking about?"

"I tell you, all of us have the same eyes," I framed one of my eyes with two fingers. I also pointed at Hecate, who had been standing in the middle of the room. "But I saw for several moments that color in those of the traitor."

"It is the mark of our great goddess," whispered Anaëlle. She took a hand to her mouth and closed her eyes. Two veins sprang from her eyebrows, creating a v shape on her forehead. "The mixture of human blood with hers."

I couldn't help to watch Bob. His eyes weren't like theirs, but they weren't like ours either. It had to be due to so much energy that he had received directly from the source. That would prevent them from being jealous of him, I said to myself. For being their great goddess' chosen one.

Their statement overwhelmed me. I knew I had not imagined what I had seen in Bayron's eyes. I receded until I found Hecate's arm; Bob had also done the same thing to get back to the security that we provided him. I felt Bruce several meters to the left; it would not be difficult to save him, if those creatures who called themselves non-humans decided to attack us.

The four siblings before me, frightened, raised their hands. Nothing in their energy indicated that they were going to set a trap for us. But if what they were saying was true, it would mean that the traitor who had taken my community to the point where it was, was no other than a descendant of Hecate. I did not try to finish her at that moment, for having committed such imprudence, only because it was as close to my community as I had near; And part of me, I didn't know if I'd ever even find my father again.

"Mmmm," murmured Monique. The sweet, ashamed look had vanished from her countenance. "You said that it was a traitor..." Her eyes flashed when she fixed them in mine.

Her sister looked at all three of us and directed her face to the place where Bruce was.

"A human on the brink of starvation," she took her hand to her chin, the v shape on her forehead had not disappeared. "Our idol accompanied by one of the fallen of the sky. As humans called them at the time," she added, to explain the change of name, "and also by a human... One of us," she corrected herself instantaneously. "You have not been able to kill that traitor that you are fleeing from," it infuriated me that she had expressed it aloud. It was our truth, but it wasn't nice that they mentioned it. "Except for you," she kept on looking at me, "it is as if they all had come out of the Great War."

"That's right," I admitted, tired of so much beating around the bush. "We're looking for something that would stop that traitor." I took my hands to my waist, ready to charge against the first one who began to raise their energy. "And being one of your own, I demand help."

If their intentions were the same as Bayron's (whatever they were), I did not think they were willing to give me his head; but, seeing how they had behaved with us, I was almost sure of their answer.

Julien had turned white. I thought he was going to lose consciousness, but the only thing that happened to him was that he was suffocated by fear.

"Please..." He begged, almost falling down the stairs. "We followed your teachings," he took one of my hands in his. I released a great exclamation when I felt his contact above the armor. "There has to be another explanation."

"Of course, there isn't!" Almost howled Anaëlle. I was surprised by the anger with which she spoke. "Sister, who has access to the vault?"

"The four of us," she hurried to answer. "And..." her eyes opened widely. We were all able to see the image that had formed in her head.

I saw that she herself spoke to Aymerick, granting her the privilege of accessing a closed room with a gigantic silver door; also, we feel her own doubt about the real reason why the female human who hated us so much, had been wandering right in the place where we were.

I came back from my absorption, when they all ran to catch her. The twins and the sisters asked us to go with them, to check what was had been stolen. And they invited us to access their minds if we doubted about their loyalty. To which of course we refused. No culprit would invite you to enter his mind in such a freeway. And less if it was a half human, or whatever those creatures were.

"What do you seek?" Dared to ask Bob, as we walked swiftly down a dark hallway.

"No one controls the comings and goings of others," said Julien. "We would like to talk to her, to see that she didn't help that person."

"Let's hope they didn't steal anything."

What if that human had helped Bayron to get one of the weapons that brought us to the red prison? I remembered Bayron fighting. He wasn't a great Hunter, he didn't even take off his armor... And he never bothered to use his energy, except for assassinating Hecate's humans. More and more it was more possible that he was one of them, hidden among our ranks.

Anaëlle and her sister held each other's hands and placed themselves in front of the vault's door. Their energy melted as if they were a single person and soon the door yielded, giving us a freeway. It was a square room, completely full of guns. Even on the roof I could observe knives and other types of contraptions; in the center of the stay was an empty place: a stone that seemed to have been burned with blue fire; it was as big as Eugène and Julien. I felt that a surplus energy, coming from what was once nailed to the stone, repelled me, burning my skin. I observed, more carefully, the hole that gave off that gleam of corrosive energy; some drawings bordered it. Useless to say that I understood what it said, accessing the higher energy that surrounded all of us, which gave me the power to understand anything. The inscriptions read «the hand of whom cannot be touched». The hole was small, narrow enough to bear the weight of a rod; and the ceiling was high enough to lodge the height of the weapon that was forming in my mind. That was the place where the great crosier of my memories was kept.

"They took the crosier of Osiris!" The dismay that was guessed in their voices was so thick that I could even feel it. "Ungrateful. Traitor! Bring her to me!"

A v shape was formed on the foreheads of the four creatures that accompanied us. Monique and Anaëlle threw themselves as an exhalation through the door. Seconds later, I heard someone shouting; it didn't take long for the smell of blood to get to us. I checked fifteen times in less than a second that Bruce was still safe. I still didn't want my mind to start thinking that the situation could get out of hand. I focused on Bruce and what was happening right then and there.

"What has she taken?" inquired Bob, admiring the empty space at the great rock. "What is the crosier of Osiris?"

He hugged Hecate delicately, whose face was frozen in an expression of terror. She did not come to herself until the soft cold of her companion's hands came to her skin; it was then that she smiled and the energy around her became of a lighter color.

Eugène looked at us from the bottom of the room, with an unfathomable look. Then he passed his eyes swiftly over all the weapons in the room. He took two knives that he had near and kept them in his pockets.

"It is the weapon which they used to locked our deities in the underworld."

An exclamation was released from my lips. I knew what had been there, but having the confirmation, made me shudder. Immediately, my mind began to bubble; I just saw ways to get away from there with Bruce. The fact of being so close to something that had been about to kill us all, disturbed me.

"With which they locked you up," seconded Julien. "We are looking for the other six relics that were used for such an outrage."

"You mean, to lock us up, the humans of that time created seven contraptions?" The tone of my voice sounded more and more like the one they used. I did not know if what Hecate had said between lines was really going to happen, by then, I was almost as frightened as a human before a big black panther.

"Holy God, of course not!" Julien left the task. He approached me with a firm step. Despite having such a sturdy body, he felt intimidated by the magnitude of mine. "Everything that was created at that time," he spoke slowly, as if he did not believe I could understand it, "was thanks to you. Had it not been for all that you taught those humans, they could have never locked you up anywhere."

"Much less in another dimension," said thirdly, another of those creatures, which had just showed up on the threshold of the room. He was thin and blond, his eyes also presented the yellow tone that so characterized them. "I'm Basil." I present my loyalty to the goddesses," he added, performing the reverential gesture that all made. "They have caught Aymerick trying to escape through the vents. Ought to be stupid," he said to himself. "We're going to let her defend herself," he sounded like he was apologizing for his people's behavior. "And then..."

"Come on, everybody!" Julien left in a box three stones and four blades. "The only thing that that bastard has stolen from us was the crosier and the ring."

"No," said Basil. "She had the crosier when we caught her."

"What a relief!"

As we walked through another of those endless halls, I went over all the events that we had experienced in such a short time with those creatures. They had confirmed to us that they were almost Hecate's direct descendants; a group that she had to leave for having suffered the first part of her transformation. As if that were not sufficiently shocking, they had to make it clear to us that, if we had seen another creature with yellow eyes, it would certainly be one of their group. Aymerick had exposed herself; even without having made it clear that she hated us, being one of the people who could open that great door was reason enough to distrust.

Hecate interrupted my train of thoughts as she suddenly stopped. Eugène collided with her, he receded almost immediately.

"What's the matter with you, now?" I snapped at her. I overlooked that she was shaking and her eyes were lost in a very distant place.

"I'm not going," she said. She took several steps backwards, "I don't want to see it again!" She squealed, curling up into a ball on the ground.

The humans tried to approach her, I stopped them with one hand. The energy that Hecate gave off at times like this could be harmful even to me. And despite being a demon, she had a great love for humans. She would never forgive herself if she ever harmed any one.

Although, on second thought, she probably would have lost count of her nocturnal murders.

"I will go alone," I informed the twins and Basil.

They shook their heads affirmatively. They resumed the march in silence. I understood Hecate's concern: to meet again with the same contraption that had locked her and had separated her from us indirectly, had to be a very strong shock. Even I, myself felt that the energy of my body moved in a different way. The piece that was missing from my puzzle, was kept suspended on me, without wanting to fit in and without wanting to go away. It was all our fault. It was an evidence that we could not overlook. Had it not been for our own knowledge, they would have never taken away what was our own.

"I do want to see it," I whispered to the three humans. They looked at me, but they didn't say anything. "I want to meet again what sent me down there."

The rage with which I spoke surrounded us all for long moments. I was furious. Confirming that my species had been solely responsible for their destruction... was too much. After all, we were not so different from humans. What would it have been that they had learned from us? How much did we teach them one day? Did we love them so much as not to see what they would surely become?

"And also, the responsible human?" Basil asked me, stopping the march slightly. "Do you also want to see the human who locked you all up?"

In spite of wishing to see the face of the person responsible for our downfall, I knew that if I affirmed my desire to rip his head off, it would be a precedent for all the human worshippers of Hecate to become wicked and to want to avenge us somehow. If I have to say something about humans, it's that they performed a lot of revenge games.

I watched the way they had to walk. Their muscles were tense with each of the steps they gave; not in the same way as Bruce's did, for he had not yet managed to reach that amount of mass muscle. At that time, he was still a thin human, almost malnourished due to our escape; soon he would look like all of them. I did not want that such beautiful energy that I had seen when I reached that place, was corrupted, as Hecate's energy had done. I wanted to keep them as pure as possible, if that was in my hand.

"No." I was surprised about how firm my voice sounded. "We've had enough blood," the echo of the aisle transported my voice away, "I just want the relic back," my boots splashed the floor, when I stepped on a puddle, "I want to snatch from them everything we gave them."

"So, everything will be like before," it seemed that Basil shared my reasoning.

"Everything will be like at first," the brothers seconded. And it almost seemed like a plea.

Chapter 11

«If it Is for Love...»

A distant whisper began to become strong in my ears. A little murmur that grew, until it became shouts of sheer rage and pain, which resonated forcefully in my head; also, the light began by a small spark. A soft and warm orange color, which seeped through a closed door. I imagined how the four of us would be seen entering in the room where so many emotions were generated. Suddenly, the doors would be opened and only the brightness of some iridescent eyes would be seen...

"It will be brief," promised Eugène.

"It's not going to hurt me to see a human suffer."

I didn't see in their faces what I expected. I saw no grudge nor anger; the shadow that crossed their faces was that of shame. They knew that he saw them as little more than humans; they knew that I would never consider them equal to me and that the fact of having found a traitor among their ranks, diluted completely any opportunity to become something more than what they were before my eyes.

I heard Basil's heart rate rise.

A part of me, a part that I tried to hide —so forcefully, that it was about to cost me more than life— wanted to make him understand that perhaps, in a few centuries, my race might come to consider them as more than mere mortals. But I didn't. I didn't even devote a look to him. All I did was to ask myself if Bruce would be tormenting himself with the same thought.

"He is no longer one of us," Basil stopped my train of thoughts. "From the moment he decided to betray everything we believed in, he is nothing but a raw mass of dead energy."

That phrase made me laugh for a lot of years.

Julien was more reserved. He said nothing at any time; he was not angry, nor anxious to see the end of all that trouble. But at the bottom of his heart, an energy almost as poisoned as that of his companions burned.

I was amazed at the size of that construction. I've never seen such a more impressive construction than our mansion. I observed the metal girders that got introduced in the rock, as if no one had put them there; as if they had always been a single thing. Maybe it was something Hecate taught them to do. I remembered her, dreamy, observing her own sculpted figure, as we walked. I could not help to release a short laughter. They looked at me with confusion, but they didn't say anything.

We were surrounded by a multitude of enraged people. From their throats emerged a vibrant murmur, as if at any moment they were going to sing a roar; they kept their eyes closed, however, they moved out of the way at our step. I walked behind the humans, to the center of the room. There was a large elevated platform, it seemed that it wasn't too worn out but, I noticed what once blood trails were.

I wondered if they made that kind of ceremonies more often than they could have admitted and a feeling similar to fear, began to grow bigger inside me. I felt again the need to measure each one of those creatures, as if it were really going to come the moment in which I had to flee with Bruce. I figured out the best way to escape that underground vault, until suddenly, I felt stupid.

Two big humans entered the room. Their black suits were darker than those of the others, their role was different. Behind them I saw

Aymerick, beaten and dirty. If I hadn't seen her that same day, I would have said that she had been hiding for months in a sewer. The humans made their way to the altar and as they approached, the murmur of their throats was rising.

The feeling of uneasiness kept on overwhelming me, swiftly, like a serpent ascending from my stomach, to my throat. I took my hand to my neck, trying to relieve the pressure.

"Sisters!" Anaëlle called out, walking with a firm step to the altar where Aymerick was. "Brethren...!" she took her hands to the heart, almost with sorrow, and extended them towards us, a gesture that made the humans boisterous. "We're here today because something has broken! Somebody has broken it! He turned the body towards the prisoner and kicked her down to the ground. "And what has broken this one..." her voice stopped with a snap. "Has broken us!"

A howl almost got me scared.

Maybe that's why Hecate didn't want to be present. She knew it. The need to talk to that girl before she was executed began to urge in me. My words would weigh on my head forever, if I couldn't get her to tell me what Bayron's plan was.

Anaëlle continued talking, while I tried to think about the best way to get close to them, without losing the unstable camaraderie that was between us. I saw Aymerick with her head down, there was no sign of that arrogance with which she had attacked Hecate. Now she was just a broken human.

I felt the twins on my back, making vibrate in their throats that infamous melody that was entering in the depths of my mind. Basil had been lost in the crowd.

I began to feel uncomfortable as the blows they gave her became a cadence of hatred and pain. Memories of similar torture were making a dent in my convictions. I wanted them to punish her for hurting Bruce; I did not care what they thought of Hecate or me or their uncertain future in El Dorado, I was only unable to remove from my mind the image of Bruce, terrified, lost in the shadows.

His lips were broken and the blood dripped to the ground, it got lost in the pores of the rock. I tried to think that she had helped Bayron to enter our world and create a source of pain; but, the chains tinkled, transporting me again to the prison... Orange memories that were lost swiftly in my memory.

Despite everything that had happened to us, I thought it was too hasty to kill her at that time, we had to know what had led her to everything they had done.

"She left us..." I heard only that lament. "No one else cared."

"Why don't you let her talk?" They didn't listen to me either.

"After using us" Anaëlle's voice resonated in my ears and stayed several seconds in the air, "after lying to us..." she entwined her fingers in Aymerick's dirty hair, to leave her neck uncovered. "Through here it is cut," she whispered, leaving a languid path in her throat.

There I realized that they were not interested at all knowing why... And I had to intervene.

"Stop!" All the humans froze, as if their hearts had suddenly stopped.

Monique appeared on the scene. She walked with a calm pace until she stood next to Anaëlle, who took her hand without looking away from me. She was so mad at me for interrupting her ritual, that she would have attacked me if it wasn't for her sister. Monique knew it; she knew that if she faced me, I couldn't hold back. And to none of them we had told the part where that wound almost left me powerless.

«Without magic», Bruce's voice crossed my ears and I inadvertently began to reassure myself.

"I want to know what both of them did," Monique held her sister's hand tightly. "I want to know how they did it!"

After an instant of reflection, which lasted too much in the case of a human, she finally articulated a word; a word that made it clear to me that her intentions were by no means close to helping us; a word that made me remember why I was in that situation...

... Because of the humans.

"No," that sentence nailed me to the ground. "No one will talk to the prisoner."

No one moved. The vibrations of their throats descended to become almost inaudible. I felt the energy vibrate in my hand and I thought about how quickly I could finish all that if I just...

"Sister," Monique's voice stopped my train of thoughts. The crowd dissipated around me, as if they were mere shadows leaving a room.

I remained motionless, unable to blink, nor to lift even the legs. I sighed. Anaëlle smiled at me before she got lost behind a door. Soon I was alone, trying to process what I had lived in that room. I had seen companions... people who claimed to be sisters, spit and yell at one of their members until they caused her tears. I had been one of the first to ask for a punishment, however, after seeing that trial, I could not help feeling bad.

I noticed a presence behind my back. Warm, soft fingers patted my forearm and gently descended into interlocking with mine. Hecate leaned her head on my shoulder, releasing a great snorting. For several moments, it did not bother me to have her so close because, for once,

I felt that our energy could be part of only one thing. At that time, we were not two confronted creatures, we simply existed in peace.

"That's why I left them behind."

That statement, however, made me lose all the peace I could have collected in several lives. Alarmed, I receded several steps. She remained still, fully aware that I would not leave without hearing more.

"What are you saying?" I asked, terrified. "If someone listens to you..."

"There is no one," she concluded. "There's nothing to be afraid of," she smiled. "They can never understand anything I say."

"Stop it!" I cried out. "You can't speak that way here!"

The expression of her face was serene, as if after centuries of keeping that, she would finally dare to say it aloud. She may have already forgotten her sinister game.

"Come," she stretched out her hand for me to take it. "Let's go back to the humans."

She took me by the hand and we walked together through those cold hallways, which had previously been full of life and were now gloomy and solitary. What had happened? Maybe they've always been like this and not how they showed us. They wanted our help that was clear to me, whether it was to use us as a door to El Dorado or to anything else.

Hecate had said that she did not know what that world was and it was indeed true; she had spent so many years here, so long believing to be a fallen goddess from the sky... It was understandable that she would have forgotten. Her bare feet transformed a puddle into a mass of black crude, the hand with which she pulled me, delicately, had the same temperature as mine. I held it hard, trying to take strength to face that new world.

"Here's Bruce," she told me. "He's been sleeping all night."

"Where are you going?" It escaped from my mouth.

She had a strange look when she looked at me, seeing how unusual my behavior was to her. At that moment, in which I expected her answer, I felt small, a speck of dust awaiting the response of a sun. Through her eyes passed several emotions and it was when I saw myself reflected when we both realized that I was afraid.

She smiled as she passed through the door, she put her hand on the doorknob, as if it were a caress. Every display of the repentant creature had vanished altogether.

"Look for me later," was the only thing that came out of her shiny mouth.

I remained silent, seeing the small gap of light that was projected from the inside. I pushed the door and saw Bruce, sitting on a blue bed, he looked dirtier than when we arrived but, he also had another color on his cheeks; the stains that surrounded his eyes were also gone: he had a different vitality.

"Bruce," the words got stuck in my mind, I soon noticed a strong pressure in my throat. I wanted to share with him everything I thought was happening around us, but he came forward to me:

"When I woke up, you weren't here!" His reproach struck me. "I thought you'd left me alone..."

That horrified me.

"Never!" I ran to him and we fused in a warm embrace, a gesture of affection so typical of Bruce. "I won't leave you alone."

Of course, he didn't see the worry in my face. He just wanted to tell me that Bob had given him the best food he'd ever enjoyed in days. (How many days?) He laid down beside me as long as he was, with his hands behind his head. He would soon be taller than Bob.

"I've been with other humans."

He almost said it with shame.

I remained silent for a moment, waiting for him to continue. Seeing that he would not continue to speak, I insisted:

"And...?"

"I didn't know it was like that..."

He felt so ashamed that I could almost see how emotions tore him up inside. He was concerned about my opinion; he was worried about disappointing me or making me angry.

"It's always nice to feel accepted," I ended up whispering. I wanted to add something else, but I didn't want to overwhelm him anymore. "It is fine."

Bruce smiled.

I heard someone coming down the hall. They walked slowly, firmly, with enough confidence to make noise. My body was slightly stressed when I heard two hard knocks at the door.

"I am sorry to interrupt," Basil entered with a paused attitude. "With all that has happened we have not been able to show you our hospitality." His smile widened to see that Bruce smiled so much. "I could escort you to the thermal baths."

"Thermal baths?" Bruce asked.

"Yes," said Basil, leaning against the door frame. "It's been a long day for everyone," he stared at Bruce and then at me. "I'd like you to feel comfortable."

An endless instant passed by until I perceived that they were awaiting my answer.

"Okay," I jumped up and walked slowly to the exit.

Bruce came after me, as energetic as it allowed him his physical state. Nothing would happen to let him relax for a few hours, I didn't want him to get sick again.

We crossed the dark corridor and passed into a chamber of gilded walls, with fine floral details that made me think of Hecate's arms. The vaulted ceiling was blurred between the shadows, the light that allowed us to see the path, came only from the torches and from a few tiny devices that formed a straight line on the ground, marking the way.

Basil came forward to indicate the way to us, because despite being signposted, the lights were divided into several paths that were lost in the dark. That fortress stretched deep into the earth; I was not the only one astonished by its magnitude, Bruce was also lost in each of the details that we found. After all, the only construction I had ever seen was that of our own house. I felt a draught going around my belly, we could not stay much more there, I had to get Aymerick to tell me how Bayron had managed to deceive us; I had to know how a couple of humans had deceived us for so long.

The rage began to furrow my cheeks, when I heard a voice interrupting my thoughts:

"I am sorry about the trial incident," I stopped for an instant, not knowing very well what he meant. "Sometimes Anaëlle is like that. We only want a punishment for those who betray us."

With that tone of voice he could almost have made me forget the trial, what really happened in that place; any other time, could have made me forget all the blood and all the hatred that came out of their bodies. If I had been anyone else or weaker, his words would have dragged my whole conviction.

My eyes passed from Basil to Bruce, who still seemed absorbed by the light mechanism guiding our footsteps. Would have they tried something like that with Bruce? I needed to be with him again, so he could tell me exactly what they had told him.

Basil was waiting for an answer.

"Blood is paid with blood," I said and I felt something writhing inside me, because even if I was capable to hate Aymerick, seeing how her brothers treated her, made me see that they were by no means how they made us believe.

While arriving to a branch of the passage, the lights turning to the left changed color and those on the right were kept the same. Bruce looked at me when Basil said I would have to go to the thermal on the other side. Neither of us liked the idea of being parted any longer but, I didn't want things between those humans and me to get tense any more.

"I'll see you later."

Basil pointed to me as a gesture where I had to continue. When I turned around, he passed an arm over Bruce's shoulder, with camaraderie.

I walked down the path to the left; as I introduced myself deep into the tunnel, I began to hear the sound of the water colliding against the stones. I thought of the sea and the pain that all those memories caused me. Soon I was wrapped in a spiral, I ran out of breath and had to grope for a supporting point. I felt the wall in my hand and I stood still, very still, waiting for all those images to dissipate in my mind: the crosier, pointing at us; my mother, drowning at the bottom of the blue abyss; Aingeru, falling into the void and the last smile that shone in my father's mouth. All of that. All that I had lost.

"Oh, come on, come on!" Cried out a voice. "Nor that it is so bad to bathe with me," Hecate released a giggle when I raised my head.

The water fell like a waterfall from the ceiling to the central pool, emanating vapors that briefly hid her body, which stood up like a statue in the center of the room. She looked like a fairy emerging from the forest. She took several leaps until she reached my side.

"Don't you think it's strange?" She asked me, staying a few steps away from me.

"What?"

She wanted a concrete answer, but at that instant my brain could not process anything.

"How are these humans!" a step closer. "What's wrong with sharing time and space? She added, as if I had not understood.

"Do they that think I don't realize that?" She smiled, pleased to see that I entered in her game. "Bruce may not see what they're trying to do..."

"Oh!" She stopped me. "Maybe, all they want is for that little kid is that he doesn't worry about anything. A trial is not the most appropriate place for a child."

"Neither is this hole. We've been on the verge of dying too many times!" I burst, as if it were her fault.

The vapor began to rise behind Hecate, as if it were a waterfall that challenged gravity.

"The truth," she began to say, "is that you have been close to die."

I rolled my eyes and sighed hard. I had to fully support my back against the wall, because she was really close. The torn sleeves of her robe caressed my legs delicately, as if they were part of the steam around us; her blue eyes shone as they got fixed into mine, like two stakes; I could not help staring at her mouth: two big pink lips, by which had passed through Bruce's blood and flesh. And how many other people? How many people had she eaten already? Her smile twisted as she realized my thoughts.

"The only thing to worry about is that this boy has hidden the gun well," I was hoping that too. "I would hate to see that they have another way of retaining you."

"They can't retain me!" What was she saying? Though deep down I knew exactly what it was.

"Of course!"

That suspicion was anchoring, forcefully, in my head, but, as it got out of her mouth, I felt even more unprotected.

I sighed.

"I am not in a hurry, neither is Bob," the humidity of the environment made her hair to stick on her face. "But you are," I didn't want to hear any more. I knew they were earning merits with Bruce but, to the point of not letting us out... "There is something you should have clear already and it is that if they have Bruce..."

I wanted answers and they wanted to silence Aymerick; I wanted to be with Bruce and they would take him away from me. It was a pulse between us and if they could get Bruce to ask me for more time, I wouldn't be able to leave him alone. If they conquered the little human, they had us both. Hecate wanted me to say aloud what was going on in the mind of both of us, but I could not bear her gaze more and tried to move to one side; she stopped my escape by dropping a heavy blow against the wall, right next to my head: she wasn't going to let me go. From her attire came out a slightly pestilent smell and the drawings of her arms made me remember all the way I was still to go to get home and rescue my father. I needed her help.

"...They got me."

She smiled, satisfied. She turned away from me and walked to the larger tub, the steam hid two more in the background. She shook her shoulders and her robe fell to the ground, though it might have disintegrated.

"Let's go!" She urged me. "We have time, but it's not infinite."

"Yes." I accepted. "Nothing bad happens for a bath."

"Of course not!" She flung her back into the water, splashing around. "I'll finally know what you're hiding under that black mass."

"It's not a mass!" I replied, observing the water-sway. "It's an armor. You should have one."

The armor was diluted heavily to form a puddle on the ground, which vanished in an instant.

"Me?" She took a leg out of the water. "I don't need an armor."

"You think you're that strong?"

"In fact," she stared at me, playing her fingers in the air, "yes," she added, making the hint to catch something. "Come on! Get in now!"

"One minute!"

I slipped my feet down the stairs, fearing to feel an electric current passing through me again. Hecate dipped her head and to me, it had not even touched my skin. It was possible that humans wanted to see if we had any weakness.

"Don't be afraid," I was surprised at how warm her voice was. She emerged cautiously, being careful not to get me wet. She raised her arms and her long blond mane fell heavily to her back. "Come with me," she took my hands carefully, making me believe she really cared about me. And even though I knew it wasn't true, I allowed myself to believe that she did.

I soon felt the water bathing my feet. What seemed already a thousand years old wound resented to that icy contact, but nothing bad happened. On the last step, when she no longer held me, a lash of pain ran from my leg to my back. I lost my balance and I collapsed heavily in her arms. I noticed something in my face, something that fluttered from the inside.

"You have a heart," I said trying to get away from her.

"That's right," she smiled and for the first time since I knew her, she didn't seem offended. "A big throbbing heart, which carries the oxygen from my lungs, to every one of my cells."

"What? You're not..."

"Human," she stopped me. "Yes, I know! And yet there you have it, throbbing frightened, by all that surrounds us, "I looked at her, without understanding. "It had been a long time without giving so much energy to Bob and..." She stopped abruptly. Well, and what came later."

I rolled my eyes and sat at the bottom of that pool, it was rough to the touch and the tiny stones were molded against my skin, as if they were gelatin.

"And will one day stop beating?"

"Who knows?" She merely responded. She untangled her hair with one hand. "Oh, heavens! I'm so dirty!"

"If you're not sure," I started to ask, even though I knew she wasn't going to answer. "Why do you lose so much energy with...?"

She laughed sharply.

"What good is immortality to me, if I cannot share it?"

She closed her eyes and got relaxed in the water. She floated with her eyes closed until she noticed I was leaving.

"Uh! Hold on!" She jumped out of the pool and took me by the shoulders. "You are not thinking about leaving me here, do you?"

"Actually, yes."

"Why isn't there any human here? Bob and Bruce, having a great fun with everyone and you and me here alone... It must be because you have upset Anaëlle," she moved away from me in a dramatic way.

"I haven't upset anyone!"

"Hey, hey! Don't worry," she took a new tunic from one of the gray-stone chairs. "Oh! What is this tunic?" The tunic was a towel. "I can't put my arms through here!"

"The clothes are there," I said, pointing out a bunch of stacked pieces. "That's to dry our bodies."

She had lived so long among humans and she was unable to differentiate a towel from a pair of trousers.

"And here I have to put my legs?" She asked me, horrified. "I don't know why you're laughing! With this you won't be able to wear your armor."

"I just need a moment to put it on. Besides," I added, "I don't want to piss off our hostesses."

I had fun in silence to see her so distressed by the clothes. I wished that was the greatest of our problems.

"Ha!" She grunted, passing a white sweater through her head. "Like you care about that. I mean, I don't mind offending them, there's a reason why I left here a long time ago."

"Why aren't you more careful?" I snapped out. I finished lifting my pants to the waist, I did some stretching to see how flexible they were and I buttoned them. "They could be hiding anywhere," I whispered, "listening. They can hide," she seemed to have forgotten how Aymerick had taken Bruce away from us.

"Perhaps I do not see them because it is part of me, which runs through their veins," she remained thoughtful for a few moments. "And you..." She fixed her eyes into mine and the memory of the sea devouring me struck my mind.

The rage drowned that image and after the pain, there was only Hecate's face, who smiled.

"That was your fault!"

She was taking me to the limit, despite being my only ally, I wanted to take her off me as soon as I could.

"Okay," she agreed. "Let me comb you, in peace" reluctantly, I turned my back on her and sat hugging my knees. She knew I had no choice but to follow her game. "And tell me, what are we going to do about humans?"

"Nothing," I pointed out. "There's nothing to be done."

"Come on, get a little closer," her hands fell heavy on my shoulders. "Let me take you away from them all."

She passed her fingers through my hair, several times, leaving languid paths along my head.

She continued murmuring for a few moments until she realized that I would not answer her and not because she had offended me, but because her caresses transported me to a cozy place, far from all that; a place that no longer existed in any universe, that faded in the deepest corners of my mind. In those moments I believed that Hecate's hands belonged to my body too, I felt a tingle going through the last pore of the skin, a strange feeling but, at the same time, pleasant. Hecate released a jumping giggle, the one that was so much typical of her. I opened my eyes and realized that nothing had changed: we both were locked still in that room covered with steam; the humans would be with Bruce still, earning his trust, taking advantage that he was weak and he felt that he did not fit with us... with me.

"That's enough," I said, getting away from her side. I observed the rough appearance of my skin and the calm smile that was attached to my face.

"It will soon be over and this," she put a hand on my arm, "would become a pleasant thing."

Those words wanted to be kind, but the meaning behind them was quite different. What she was telling me was not something I was willing to listen to. At least, not at the time.

"Shut up!" I jumped up. I pushed her hands away with a stronger blow than I intended. "Nothing has started!" She said nothing, she just stood silently. "So, nothing will be over!

"Your world is being demolished and there is only a great abyss at your fee. Decide if you are going to jump or let it smash you!"

I turned my back on her and walked away quickly. I was fed up with all that: of humans with their intrigues; of Bruce letting himself be deceived and especially of her, who thought she knew everything. I went out into a dark hallway, fearing that at any moment she would appear by my side. Although nothing happened. I remained standing in that place, the only thing that seemed to accompany me were the little lights of the ground that turned off behind my back and began to mark me a path in the gloom.

I sighed.

I began to follow the yellow lights, with the sole purpose of getting away from Hecate and also with a slight touch of curiosity. I wondered what mechanism would be turning them on and why they would want to drive me anywhere. I allowed myself a moment to think about Bruce but, I couldn't break into the pools saying they were manipulating him. I walked through several gloomy and cold passages, there were areas in which the drippings were seeping, which ended up forming small black puddles. While walking alone in those places, I realized that it was just old stone, there was no trace of the golden nuances, or the warm feeling of being on the clouds. It was all lies; everything was delusions. The lights led me to the grand trial hall, I passed by the central stone, I watched closely the streams of blood that had already faded over time. I grazed with one hand the surface and I felt a shiver before death. Those human hid too much. I saw the door by which they had taken Aymerick's motionless body and I ran. It was clear that they would not allow me to speak to her before executing her.

The door was small and it was closed, it had numerous scratches, it seemed that the prisoners had put all their efforts not to enter. They would surely know that whoever came in here would never enjoy freedom again. I used part of my energy to open it, without leaving flaws, I did not want to realize the effort to carry out such a simple task. I went downstairs cautiously, as if something were to attack me from one moment to the other. There were no beams that held the structure, it was a simple hole in the stone, even deeper than the others. That basement was divided into small cages that came to the ceiling, where there was a small opening, where they would feed them, I guessed. There was a lot of silence, it was almost sticky, the tense atmosphere that precedes disasters. The cages had openings large enough for the prisoners to pull out their arms. Had it been full, it would have cost me to get to the bottom of the tiny hallway, fortunately for me, there was only one prisoner.

Aymerick was sitting against the wall, her face even more swollen and red, it was not at all like the sardonic and jaded gesture with which she received us.

"Well!" So, there she was, after all. "I thought you were bringing me food," she stretched until her back creaked. "But you assassins don't eat."

"I don't think I'm the only assassin in this room," I said, giving in to her provocation.

She looked askance at me and laughed.

"I know why you're here. You think I'm going to tell you something?" She did not wait for me to speak to continue. "You know everything there is to know."

"No!" I shouted, tired already. "I don't know anything. One way or another you'll tell me what I have to know!"

She didn't seem frightened. She got up with difficulty and came up to me.

"They won't let you make me talk," she smiled, even though she lacked teeth. "They're so happy to have you here that, they will barely want to pay attention to me. And the sooner you forget the incident of my treachery, the sooner you will give them what they want."

"What they want".

"How were you able to deceive us?" I mumbled, without wanting to hear anything else, "how?"

"Just as a child is deceived," it was her only answer. She kept her eyes fixed on mine, yet I could see a glimpse of fear.

I gave a blow against the bars, the metal vibrated for several moments. She receded frightened, same as satisfied. Even having the certainty of being executed, what pleased her the most was to know that we were more lost than before we found them. Her words had not mitigated my anguish, they had only confirmed one of my fears: as soon as she disappeared and the winds of treason had vanished, I would have to give them something in exchange... in exchange of what? They had not given me any answer, they had only created more questions. That's why they wanted Bruce on their side, in case I decided not to help them.

François came running, fearing that I was about to assassinate her. I could hear him even before he came into the trial room. I walked away from her before the footsteps began to resonate at the top of the stairs.

"What are you doing here?" He asked me. He stopped half way from the cell. I was pleased that he was still afraid. "We're not authorized to talk to the prisoners."

"You are not authorized," I hissed and words lacerated my mouth, "human."

I dedicated one last look to Aymerick, who smiled. I passed without even seeing François, without paying attention to his poor weapons or to his tremors. With one foot on the stairs, I gave him some last words:

"You smell like death already."

When I went upstairs again, I saw Hecate sitting on the stone. Her attitude made me think for a moment that it was not about her, because I saw her so relaxed that it simply could not be about her. She had one foot resting on the edge and she rocked the other absent-mindedly in the void, until the moment in which she saw me. The demonic essence that made her who she was ignited inside her again. She smiled.

"You look like a human," I told her as I approached her.

"Do I look like one?" She answered me, amused. "Maybe I am."

She jumped at my side and led me to the gates, just at the moment when they got opened to make way to Anaëlle and Monique, who were holding hands.

"Oh!" said Monique. "I knew you wouldn't fail us!"

Hecate was slightly behind my back, I was not thrilled to be used as a shield.

I nodded lightly. Anaëlle did not seem pleased at all.

"I hope you have rested enough," she strove to hide the resentment that was beating inside her. Her heart skipped a beat when she stared at Hecate closely. "I am pleased that the clothes have been of your liking. Red suits you well."

We were invited to walk to the place reserved for the most important members of that community, close enough to the great stone to see the blood running; far enough to see it without twisting one's neck. They went up and began to speak among whispers, as if for getting away we were unable to hear them.

"I don't want to see what's going to happen," she seemed really nervous. "I shouldn't have waited for you."

"Then why did you do it?"

I was beginning to get fed up with her incomplete comments but, when I was about to add something else, Bruce appeared followed by Basil and Bob. His face was lit up when he saw me and immediately he was right in my arms. I was frightened to recognize how much I had missed him.

"Have you been treated well?" I asked him. He had wet hair and he gave off a smell of flowers, really nice.

"A lot!" He recognized. He must have seen something in my face, for he hastened to add: "but it has not been the same without you. Even without you, witch."

Hecate looked at him long and fell into Bob's arms. She whispered something in his ear and that was indeed impossible for me to hear. I tried to force my energy to understand what they said to each other but, I noticed a slight pressure on the thigh and the sudden fear of feeling the pain again.

"They told me it was her fault," Bruce told me, when they dragged Aymerick out.

"What's her fault? Bruce."

"She hurt me," that statement, however, surprised me. "And it's also her fault that my brother is..."

They had had plenty of time to talk to him. I wondered what else they would have told him. I wanted to get Bruce out of there as soon as possible.

I saw the sisters talking to all of us; I also saw the way they used to push the prisoner to the ground. In one of those shoves, Aymerick's face struck against the rock, which produced the first stain of blood. That stone seemed to suck greedily the life that escaped from it. Everything began to close around me, I knew that Bruce was by my side, but if he had not been, I could have heard that throbbing heart at any distance. He didn't want to admit it, but he was scared. And so was I. We all shared a silent fear which we would never talk about.

Aymerick was offered the opportunity to talk about her crimes, something she vehemently rejected, as if she had been preparing that answer for a lifetime. She didn't care about telling us everything, it didn't matter now, if she was going to die anyway?

Bruce slowly approached me, maybe unconsciously, or perhaps it was I who approached him. I felt the energy traversing Hecate's body and mine own beating deep, very deep. I wondered if I would be able to use it if the time came. My eyes were fixed in the sisters, specifically, in Anaëlle, the contrast offered by both was as evident as the fact that it was she who controlled them all, since she did not approach while her sister was beating Aymerick; her hands were not stained with blood, she simply let them rest on her belly. Something dark was visible through her eyes; when she heard her prisoner's refusal, she smiled. It was her the one who didn't want us to know anything, but if she wanted that I helped her getting into El Dorado, why didn't she want me to know? Her head turned slowly until she found my gaze squarely and it was at that time that I knew, that she knew I would leave with everyone as soon as I had the occasion, and if keeping the unknown, would assure her a place of control over me, she would try it.

I had to show her that she couldn't make with us everything she wanted; I had to show Bruce that judging your brothers without giving them a chance to speak, was just a matter of the humans of the past; I had to prove to him that he shouldn't be like that.

I got away from them and walked slowly. I hoped it would not be necessary to get closer; I hoped that it would only be necessary the energy that I managed to accumulate. Anaëlle looked at me, as if noticing what I was about to do, but without believing it, I suppose. Her sister put Aymerick on her knees, her chin was very close to the edge of the stone. Bruce released an exclamation when the sword flashed into the hands of one of the twins, after all, he was nothing but a kid.

"I never wanted to..." mumbled Aymerick. "I never meant to hurt you," she ducked her head. "All I wanted was for them to leave!" She wanted to leave this world with rage, not as something broken. "You're far from understanding what happened and what's going to happen. All of you! You won't be ready..." She released a nervous laughter. Monique took the sword with both hands, her muscles tightened under her clothes. "If it's for love," I raised my arm and let the energy go through my skin. A beam of light passed through Aymerick's body before the sword found its destiny. We had time to hear her last words: "God allows it."

Chapter 12

«The Brightness of Memories»

Aymcrick had a tragic ending, as much as her last hours had been. No one remained, except for those responsible of getting rid of it and us.

I watched the black robes that hid their faces as they lifted the body. The wound of the energy blow that had killed her was still smoking. I had twitched my hand around Bruce's arm, fearing that at any moment they shot me. At that time, I did not think about how one of their blows would be, as they were not at all as they seemed.

Hecate stayed by my side, she was not worried about Bob's reaction or the reprisals they might have against us. All she did was stand there, looking at nothing, lost in the same way I was lost.

"Bruce..." I meant to say, but nothing came out of my mouth.

I released the pressure from his arm and continued to observe the frenzy with which they treated Aymerick's lifeless body. What was it that had led her to commit the stupidity of stealing that contraption, in the presence of all? She was definitely desperate, but why?

They prepared the bonfire in the center of that same room, a great pyre that would burn all night. A horrible death and a worse ending. She should have not been executed underground, so far from the open sky, they should not leave her remains there, either. I looked at the ceiling and suddenly, I felt my feet touching thousands of dead bodies, stretching their black hands towards me.

The flames' sizzling was replaced by some shouting.

The four of us looked towards the noise and then to ourselves, hoping that it would be someone else who broke the silence. It would be she who spoke first, keeping quiet was not at all something that had to do with her and she had been quiet for a long time.

"I almost feel sorry for that kid.

"If they hadn't found it..." lamented Bob. "But how not to attend the funeral of his beloved one."

"His beloved one?" I asked.

"How not!" Seconded Bruce.

No one deigned to answer me. It was as if they shared an evidence, which for me was imperceptible. And what would I know about love at that moment; how could I have known nothing of their relations and their complicated words, if it was all as easy for me as to feel the wind? After all, Bruce was the only human with whom I had shared my life and was he the one who insisted on naming everything.

I sighed and allowed myself to stop listening to those shouts.

"They must want an accomplice."

"So that everyone is calm..."

"And their little world will become almost the same," Hecate put a slight emphasis on the word «almost». The strength of her voice increased and I saw how all the grief she felt vanished. "Now they have something else."

"Not for long!" I was surprised of saying it, utterly exalted.

The three looked at me, with the same astonishment with which I listened to myself. Something in the environment was tense and urged the people of the tunics to leave the place, leaving the body to our care.

"What?"

"We have to go!" The words came so fast out of my mouth, as they did from my head. "Don't you see what's going on? How can you be so blind?"

Bob's eyes were widely opened.

"Calm down!" Bruce raised his arms, with the clear intention of touching me.

I swatted him away.

"No! I can't!" I took my hands to my head. Something was exploding inside me, something that had long been beating, hidden in me. "Maybe my whole family is dead". Or worse, I thought. "And I had a chance to know why!" It resounded to the depths of the flames, as slowly as Aymerick's flesh was melting.

"Why?" Inquired Bruce, flaunting his stupidity.

"You can't be that dumb," Hecate intervened. "There are here…"

"Why do you keep talking?" Bruce burst. I could see the fury in his eyes.

"Stop it! That's enough!" Bob stood between them, like so many other times. We were too many people at that instant. "You can't go on like this…" his face shrank into a grimace when Bruce raised his hand and pointed to his wound. "You are all I have left…"

Hecate gave a jump, she opened her mouth to speak, but it was Bruce who came forward:

"It's not true! You only have her and before we got here I had her!" He added, pointing at me with a certain tone of fatigue that alarmed me. "My brother hates me and we've all been broken, but now we can be a part of this!" That statement surprised us all.

"We will not be a part of anything," hissed Hecate, wanting to hit him. Even Bruce would be able to notice it in her energy. "You're a fool. A blind, deaf human kid who is determined in wanting to cut his hands and feet. And you..." She went on, wanting to say something to me. "Get ready."

"Bruce," I began to say, when she turned her back on us to leave. "Don't blind yourself. She's right, they just want to..."

"Oh! Now she's right," he stopped me. "Since when?"

"Since your friends are hiding information from us."

"What information?"

"They promised to tell us how this whole mess had happened, in exchange for the door to the other world and they didn't even allow Aymerick to speak."

"I see," he mumbled. "Maybe they don't know," he concluded, shrugging his shoulders.

I receded several steps. I lost my mind for a moment while listening to the sounds that produced the bonfire, that cave had some ventilation system that we did not see, because otherwise, we would be choking. Maybe that would allow part of her ashes to reach the sky.

"They do know," I claimed, "if not, why did they make the deal in the first place?"

That's what I had planned. I didn't have the slightest idea of how to open any door.

"If you distrust them so much," he put his arms akimbo, "after they saved my life, why don't you come into their minds?" Something broke in me. "After what you did before," he continued, pointing to the body, "I'm sure you can do it."

I lost my balance and I got staggered until I hit one of the beams at the bonfire. I turned away quickly and hid my hands, Bruce hurried to try to grab them. I felt that the whole universe was falling on me, something bad was happening in my mind, all over my body: my energy was flickering, I could hardly control it; and I had forgotten that I could touch the souls of all creatures to know more... Something was happening to me; something that had entered in my organism and was destroying it. Perhaps that is what Hecate meant, maybe that was what was happening: I would transform into an unstable and hungry creature, oblivious to all kinds of reasoning... thirsty.

"Angelyne!" I heard screaming. "Answer me!"

I saw Bruce's worried face, reddened by anxiety, and then he was covered in blood, under the moonlight. He was lost and alone in a world in which everything was a danger to him and even I, who was the most concerned about his integrity, would make me a monster.

"Go away!" I shouted, pushing too hard. He stumbled upon his feet and hit squarely to the ground. "I am sorry!"

I left Bruce there, frightened and alone, in the company of the body of a person whom I had killed. I ran aimlessly, trying to set in order everything I felt and everything that was going through my head: a multitude of images of my happy life in the great house, the perfect moment before everything fell apart... before Bruce.

I let myself fall silently in a dark and quiet corner, from one moment to another those thoughts would be lost. I took my hands to my face and felt it was wet. When I got up, frightened by the vision of the tears, I struck squarely against one of the rocks that protruded from the wall. The rock disintegrated with a small moan and fell scattered all over the floor. The yellow lights turned on again, like called by a mysterious voice that wanted me to watch, in depth, what surrounded me. I was in a narrow corridor, possibly the same by which we had accessed that infernal cave. It was then that an imperative need lit in me, with the same strength that were shining the stars that I did not see for a long time. I had to go up to the surface. Thus, perhaps, I could manage to put in order all the ideas that crowded in me and the fear of changing... becoming a demon, would disappear in the same way that it came.

Already at the end of the hall, knowing that it was indeed the door through which we had entered, I could almost feel the soft caress of the air on my skin. Unfortunately, this feeling did not last long: next to the wrecked train there were seven humans, lined up. They tried to control their heart rate when they saw me, but even so, it got altered. I approached my mind to theirs, without any regard, after having forgotten, I would make sure not to lose more energy.

I walked decisively, as if seeing them did not change my plans or, as if I did not understand why they were there. One of them got stiff, trying to get on his guard, his voice trembled more than he would have liked when he spoke:

"Halt! Stop!" I did a few meters away from him. "This area is forbidden for all residents."

"Residents? I'm not a resident!"

He interposed his weapon between both of us. Faced with the fear of being shot like Bayron, after knowing that it was from that place where he had taken the gun, I calmed down.

"We just follow orders," I noticed what they looked like, they were totally opposite to the twins, those guards seemed to be on the verge of breaking, "please..."

They had sent them there to die. Anaëlle wanted to know how far I was willing to go to get out. As if I really needed to walk to do so, or as if those guards were a problem for me. Although they just wanted to give me a message.

"Okay," I gave in, suddenly tired. "I'll talk to Anaëlle."

Their bodies were suddenly relaxed, the critical moment had already passed. I came back into the hallway illuminated only by those lights. Suddenly, I felt anger inflamed my chest and the desire to turn them off forever. I raised my hand but nothing happened, the anger intensified when I realized that I could not extinguish them with my energy. I started running away from those tiny dots on the ground. I wanted to get to the place where Anaëlle rested, I could see it even though I was so far away.

The rage seemed to feed my power, though not as much as I would have wanted but, at that moment I thought I would rise gradually, until it reached the yore point. Her room's door was opened, the only guards were the twins, who smiled at me.

"Good night, ma'am."

"Tell her to come out!" Eugène frowned and shook a leg, his muscles tightened almost as much as his face did, he was trying to scare me. "Come on!"

"There's no need to be so upset" Anaëlle came out cautiously, almost as if she was afraid, but I knew pretty well that she wasn't and less walking next to Bruce, he was his magic amulet against me.

Seeing him at her side produced two impulses in me: rip her head off her shoulders and see how Hecate devoured her. I had to strive to remain calm, the unstable calm that I could keep, so as not to scare Bruce.

"I have not been allowed to leave," I began. I leaned against a wall, trying to look calm. "If I am a prisoner, it is imperative that it is communicated to me."

"A prisoner? Don't say that!" She past an arm behind Bruce's shoulders. "You're our guests here. The new guards are here to protect you from..." She swallowed saliva.

"From Bayron," I concluded. Those guards wouldn't have been able to protect us from anything. "The traitorous human who robbed you and employed it to destroy my family. If he really stole it."

An exclamation arose from the mouths of everyone. The environment was tense and it got loaded with such a sharp energy that it choked us.

"No! He's the only culprit! We're safe here!"

It seemed like Bruce had wanted to say that for a long time. He ducked his head and hid behind that woman. That would happen sooner or later: he wanted to stay with the humans, who were like him. He wanted to be in a place where he felt one more. How could I blame him for wanting to belong to that? Or, for wanting to get away from me? After all, it was me who had killed them all.

"My father..." I stammered. "My father is still there, in the house," the twins also looked away. Only she kept on looking at me. "I'm not going to stay here while he is with him."

I turned around to leave them alone, but Anaëlle still didn't finish our talk.

"Wait." I didn't turn to face her immediately. "If you decide to leave, you can use the crosier."

That did make me look at her.

"What?"

Bruce was exultant. The food, the clothes, the rest, the medicines and that they gave me a sincere help... All that made him happy.

"If..." she turned away from Bruce and walked until she was at my side. "If you're going to face him, you have to have all the help you can get. And I promised to give it to you", she stood right in front of me. Only I could see her face, her yellow eyes which, were so similar to those of Bayron.

"No," I gave in, trying to make eye contact with Bruce. "I don't forget. You wanted to help us... Help me," I corrected, leaving Bruce aside. "In exchange for something."

She smiled.

"Bruce can stay with us," she said, waiting for him to say something. "It's dangerous for a kid to go to such a war. "And when you get back to your father, we can be together forever. Humans and Gods."

There was her feverish desire. Hecate was right, they wanted a new goddess. If I managed to defeat him, I would return to look for Bruce, triumphant, with the head of the creature who had dared to laugh at them. So, she could enact that anyone who dared to betray them, would suffer the gods' wrath.

"Is that what you want, Bruce?" I asked him, yearning for him to pray on me again, as that time when everything exploded.

"Here..." he placed his hands behind his back. "Here is not that bad. Besides I am not immortal and I do not want to die," we remained silent for a long time and he ended up adding when I was leaving: "Nor that you die."

After all that had happened there, he still cared about me. I would leave, trusting that everything would go well and hoping that, on my arrival, everything would continue to be like until that moment: Bruce and me.

"I'll take what I need," I said. I started to feel a strong pressure on my cheeks. "Make sure that the door is opened for me."

I could not bear that feeling anymore, I turned my back on them and closed my eyes hard, I just wanted to be led away from there...

...Away from everything. I noticed the floor at my feet and I watched the place I had transported to. The first thing I saw was Hecate's face, sculpted with a serene expression, a perfect face that led the way to take to a whole community of humans... If that's what they were.

I sighed and I was glad to have proved to Anaëlle that I still had power left.

Some bells rang in the distance. They chimed with a slow and growing cadence. It was a soft and beautiful rhythm... it would have been if it were any other creature. I walked to the place where the guards would be. Now there was only one wagon. I still had no crosier in my possession, nor any of those other elements that they wanted me to use but, if it was a human, I didn't need them to finish it. It was the only way to know what it really wanted. Maybe if I did what Hecate said, we could go all three of us anywhere in the world.

I closed my eyes and I got carried away by the image that his mind offered me, if there came my end, I hoped that, at least, Bruce could keep the light inside and that he reminded me with affection.

It was daylight and the sun was shining brightly, its rays were seeping through the leaves of the trees, which covered the subway entrance in which Bruce had been kidnapped. Bayron was sitting on a rock, a few meters away from me. That was the distance that I should not overcome. He stretched his legs as he saw me, with a paused attitude. We watched each other closely: he no longer wore the red cloak of my memories, nor the Hunters' armor, now he looked like a normal human. He wore trousers similar to those that had been given to Hecate and me and a blue jacket that hung open on both sides of his body.

"You don't even try to hide those eyes anymore," I hissed, wishing to throw a burst of energy that would destroy his body in thousands of pieces.

"What else should I hide?" He answered, yielding to my provocation.

"That you're tired," I added, pointing at the rock. "And that the armor no longer accepts you."

He leaned backwards, his blond curls fell on his back like a waterfall, I thought they wouldn't look the same when his head was separated from his body.

"You should not be so interested in what seems or does not," he said, he raised his arm, turned into a fist and struck it against the nearest tree, which was cracked. "You should worry about how little time your father has left," he fixed his amber look in mine and waited for my reaction.

"You bastard! All this time...!"

"Stop!" He made a gesture with his hand, so I would not come any closer. "I don't want you to be that close. Clearly, I need something from you, but unless you're willing to give it to me, I don't want to be so close to someone..." He stopped to correct himself. "Something like you."

«Something like me», those words resonated for several moments in my head. I noticed that there was no animal around us, our energies made them flee. I didn't know if I should flee too.

"I have not betrayed my own," though a part of me thought I did. "Instead, you've made those madmen kill someone who was trying to help you destroy us. You're the worst of us!"

He released a laughter.

"We're not going to play that, not today. You say those people down there are crazy," he jumped up. "And indeed, they are. Some fools who weep for what a demon taught us, instead of seeing the opportunity that exists in the simple fact of being subjected to nothing," he posed his hand on the bark of the tree. "While they wept, I learned to steal the energy that has turned me into this," he pointed to himself. "You call me a traitor, but I'm more than that," he made the trunk turn into pieces. "I am something more than the plunder of a bored god! Even" he allowed the word to float in the air, "I'm stronger than all of you!" All the trees exploded, I could see it at the moment he left his energy out. It passed like lightning through the Earth until it hit the roots that now also fell. "You have been saved by the same creature that turned them into that," he pointed to the ground, I don't know whether referring to the dust or the people hiding below. "I will thank her when you bring her to me," I looked at him with strangeness. "It is a gift that I grant you: After curing your father's wound, you will give to me all your energy and you will proclaim me King of all creatures. I will be the sovereign of this world!"

Stealing our power had made him lose his mind. I couldn't give him my absolute energy, or anyone else's. No one has never used more power than it could be stored. There was something different about him, something different to that madness, he looked more fragile but at the same time I felt that he had increased. Maybe what I saw at that moment was his human side. I wanted to convince myself that he had simply lost his mind, believing that he could dominate all of us.

"It doesn't work that way," I said, finally. "I can't show up and say you're the one who controls everything," waited a few moments. "You don't understand."

"I'll get your pet out of there," he lifted his finger in the air, enjoying of what was his joker. "I'll get him out of that place without him knowing it was for you. I will let him think that they are the vile creatures that infected his brother with suicidal ideas... When I tell him that they drove him to madness, he won't want to leave your side again."

The idea was introduced into my mind like a dagger in the flesh. It was all I wanted. My father, Bruce and I, together... Our life in the big house could come back. We'd be safe again. At the bottom of my reverie, I found myself wondering, "How does he know?" How did he know about Bruce's decision?

I raised my head to the sky, the sun shone high, immutable. How I would have liked to be like the sun at that moment!

"No..." my voice faltered and I feared to look like some of those guards who were not able to look me in the eye. "You're not going to understand anything because you're an empty, blind, stupid human who wouldn't be able to see how they spit in his face, because he's too busy trying to be something he doesn't even understand," his quiet countenance was getting altered. I could see the fire shining in his pupils. "You are not stronger than us, you are only a human traitor with longing to be..." I couldn't help but to release a laughter. "To be something like me."

"You think so?!" He shouted, leaving less space between us. "I'm going to show you how wrong you are!"

I saw how he made the gesture to take something that he kept in his jacket and as if it were a whip, the fear of pain forced me to jump on him, even knowing that it would be difficult for me to finish that fight. We rolled several meters on the ground, there was no tree that could stop our fall and we ended up hurling on a hillside. I wanted to call my armor, it had been a mistake not to have it. Without the protection it offered me, the blows were more real. I grabbed his head with both hands and smashed it into the ground, but that blow didn't work, it just seemed to hurt him. I slipped my hands frantically on him, wanting to find the weapon he intended to use against me and at least use it to stun him but, I did something better: I got to fall on him with a stone in his hand. I heard a shout that was transformed into the most beautiful thing I had heard for a long time. He pushed me hard and got up stumbling.

Something warm covered my hand with which I had beaten him. His yellow eyes showed a truth as terrible as true:

"If you bleed, you can die."

Despite my words, Bayron smiled, he turned a little away from the one that fell down his face and licked himself, slowly, enjoying the taste of his mortality.

"No!" I shouted, feeling that he was leaving. "Come back!" I yelped, but he had already dematerialized before my eyes. "You have to tell me why..."

I stayed several minutes in that place, dejected. However, seeing the dry blood in my hand, I felt strong again. We were still not finished, we could get everything back.

Swollen of satisfaction, I hastened to tell Bruce. I ran through all those halls, missing the presence of those annoying yellow lights. I was led by the heat of an orange light that was visible at the distance, I had not got so deep in that place and had not been for the excitement I felt, and I would have been more concerned.

As soon as I got out of the cave, I came to a small cliff from which you could see a large city carved in stone, which got extended along a large vault much larger than that of the trial. I could even see that they had a large lake of transparent waters. That community had been living down there for many years. I looked at Hecate and Bob jumping with unconcern over some nearby rooftops, I wanted to get close so they would tell me where Bruce was and to tell them what had just happened.

I was still overwhelmed by the fight, so I thought that stepping out of the way was going to be the best option. As soon as I went down a step that would take me to the lower part of town, a child appeared in my way. He was dirty and scruffy, he was too thin and he gave off a terrible smell. I felt the desire from a very deep place to tear him up, but suddenly I remembered Bruce: a little human child who hid from me.

"I have..." stammered the child. "I have this for you", he pulled a very bright black box out of his pocket. I was surprised that he had something so clean. "He had asked me to deliver it to you."

Bruce was so sweet, I said to myself. He wanted to put an end to our discussion with a gift. The boy opened the box and pulled out a black ring that seemed to be too small for my fingers. I stretched my hand to receive it, believing that this way, he would erase part of all the damage that I had done to them. For an instant I saw his face and I withdrew my hand before touching each other, but he was replaced by Bruce's and finally I took the ring.

"Thank you!" He shouted.

I watched him, slightly surprised, as he ran downstairs, to get lost in the maze of houses. I did not give it more importance and I tried to insert Bruce's ring on my index finger, which was too wide, I tried it in all of them and it only fit in the annular. The ring was quite wide, of a black darker than that of my armor, it contrasted with the red of the blood, which seemed to make shine the stone that it had embedded in the center, protected by two crossed bands. It was a very nice ring. I glanced at the stone that seemed to be moving in a slow red swirl...

"Angelyne!" I heard screaming at the bottom of the aisle that had taken me there. "You are there!"

Still today I do not know if having continued observing what was happening with that stone, could have done something for me. I don't know what would have happened if Bruce's voice hadn't broken my reverie.

I felt his heartbeats as he approached. Both our hearts skipped a beat when we took our hands. It was the first time I touched him that way, without there being anything between us. At that moment everything seemed to shine more, I could have sworn that we were flying through the stars, that a quiet sky was waiting for us somewhere and that none of the horrors we had passed, had really existed.

"I had to find you before you left!"

"Well, I left," I said, removing a lock of hair on his face.

"What?" He inquired. "But..."

"Never mind," I held his hands tightly, "I am here."

He smiled and his light brought to my mind the distant echoes of all those good moments; of those happy instants that we would soon enjoy again.

"I didn't want you to go without me!" He let go pell-mell.

Those words brought me back to Earth at once.

"What are you saying?"

"It's true!" I looked into his eyes, reddened by the weeping. "She told me that if I didn't say it, they would hurt you! That I had to stay with her until you left, if not, she wanted them to use one of the guns against you!"

"Oh, heavens!" I cried out, feeling the danger that we were running there. "Did they hurt you?"

"No," he lied. He turned his gaze away. "You can't touch the crosier. Or anything that has to do with it."

I started to feel a tingling in my hand.

"Why not? I need it to..."

"No," he repeated, shaking his head with fatigue. "Now it is..." he stopped, to search for the proper word, "turned off. Everything is turned off!" he raised his arms to say it more emphatic. "And if you touch it..."

"...They will hurt us."

"They don't know what will happen if Hecate touches it, but they think that if you do it, they'll be activated and so they could dominate the world."

I rolled my eyes. Everyone wanted something they couldn't have.

"Let's find Hecate and Bob! I have to tell you something, and then we'll take care of that."

"Is your hand bleeding?" He inquired, alarmed.

"Oh, no!" I hastened. "Bayron is... Ah!" I couldn't bear the sudden pain I felt in my hand.

The ring was as red as blood, I bent over my knees, trying to bear the pain.

"What's the matter?"

"It's the ring!"

Bruce tried to take it from me, but he could barely keep his hand on it. He passed an arm down my back, ready to try it one more time. I momentarily felt the warmth of his body next to mine. A cozy feeling that freed me from pain, at least for a few moments.

I heard a distant hiss, a little murmur that crawled on the rocks. I looked at the ceiling that stood above us, nothing seemed out of place. I tried to call my armor again, hoping that with it, all those annoying sensations would disappear. First came the purple glow, that overwhelming radiance that we knew so well, then came terror and explosion.

I jumped up, with my hand hiding my wounded finger, very close to my chest. Bruce was terrified, he kept his eyes stuck in the hole by which the Hunters were accessing. They could not continue obeying him. They had to know that Bayron was just a human with delusions of grandeur. A human who was going to kill us all.

Chapter 13

«Black Soul, Black Hand»

"Quickly!" squealed Bruce. The dust came swiftly to our place. Soon the Hunters would appear. "We have to help them!" Our hands were still intertwined when he started running. I let him go a few centimeters away, but I kept firm in the same place. The bewilderment that grew in his eyes traversed the exact distance that measured our extended arms, until it reached mine. "Why don't you move?"

"Bruce," I said, calmly. At least all that I could have in that situation. "We can't go," he opened his eyes widely and tried to get away from me. I closed my fist harder, so he couldn't get it. "They can't be saved anymore! Look at them!" The columns of smoke were rising everywhere, cries and tears bounced off the walls, making it seem that their souls were broken, lost. "If we go in there, we'll die! Or worse..." I swallowed saliva "they could capture us!"

"Why would they want to capture us?"

"Bayron wants us alive!"

He ceased his endeavor to free himself from my hand. He stood a few moments still, looking at nothing, until something shone inside him. How I wish I could have more time to explain everything to him!

"Is that his?" He asked, looking at my hand.

"Yes!" I claimed, vehemently, believing he spoke of the dry blood that adorned part of my arm. "We can defeat him!" as long as they were entertained defending themselves, we could get to the weapons. "We just..." I added, regretfully. "We just have to get out of here."

"How can you...?" He began to ask, with the reproach painted on his face. "If you want to leave, go ahead. Do it!" That time I was the one who let go of his hand. "I'll stay here, fighting for people who have had nothing to do with this. You can go find him alone! That's the only thing that matters to you."

He ran downstairs, by the same place the boy of the ring had gone. I didn't even have time to react.

"I only think of ourselves! That's all I care about! You'll only find death down there!"

I controlled the frequency of my breathing. I tried to take off the ring in an act of frustration with Bruce, but it seemed to be ingrown. I heard a few steps behind my back, I turned slowly, fearing to scare another frightened child. I was hoping he was only running away from the battle, that he wouldn't have any contact with me.

He raised a weapon with weak, trembling arms. He was afraid and he wanted to kill me. He might know who I was and he was wrongly relating me to the Hunters who were sweeping them.

"Don't do it," I said, I might be afraid of being hurt. "I'm not going to do anything to you."

"You are lying!" He howled.

His fingers pulled the trigger tightly and when the bullet came out of the gun, right on the trajectory I was in, a familiar hug slipped through my body, a warm mist that protected me. I felt a slight prick, like a loose stone falling out of sheer inertia. A stone that bounced off my body and returned to hit to that child, who had no protection whatsoever. His gaze was lost in a distant place, I hoped it would be a happy one; his body rushed to the ground, resembling the shell of an empty fruit. A lifeless child. A child who was afraid and just wanted to protect himself.

With the armor, the pain vanished, my hand was well, intact, as if that ring had never burned my skin; but the guilt was still there. The irrefutable truth about my true nature, was reflected more with the glow of the black material that covered my body. I always knew that, but while I had a place in Bruce's world, I didn't want to see it. I decided to lock the monster in a very deep hole, not knowing that all the monsters end up coming out.

I beheld the hard image that lay before me: a dead child at my feet, a city on fire and a war that I could finish... Everything could end there if I just told him what he wanted. A Hunter flew near, too busy projecting his energy against humans, to see me. For a few moments, the environment was transformed into another image that I had already lived: I transported to the roof of a building, a building that I would never see, nor to touch again; the Hunters wore their armor under the clear sky, deadly and silent, as beautiful as a lightning. The same image at different times, the difference was that the Hunter whom I wanted to see was already dead. It was likely that at that point everyone was dead.

I observed once more the child's body, it didn't seem to have been a soul within him. I could have thought that he had always been lying there, with a black hole in his head. He could have had blond hair instead of chestnut; he could have been in the hidden room of a big house... It could be Bruce. I stopped for a moment. I started breathing very fast. That's what could happen to Bruce! I couldn't stand there while he was in danger!

I rushed downstairs. It was like entering a totally different universe, in which there was only death. I threw my head back, feeling the desire to return but, the vision of the dead child urging me to continue, made me not wanting to look back.

Many of the houses were ruined or in flames, the cries came from every corner. "No, please!" "Help me!" I had to strive not to let those words make a dent in me, it was the first time in the battle that I felt sorry for them. I spent many alleys and crossroads, fearing that each one would be the last step I took. An explosion threw me inside one of the houses. I hastened to the outside, before they wrapped it in flames.

The street I went out to was calm, a false stillness that preceded a storm of purple clouds. I dodged several bodies that were piled on the ground, I stopped for a moment to check that it was not Bruce because, of the creatures that I was looking for, he was the most likely to die. I stepped on a myriad of pools of blood that evaporated in contact with my armor, I stared for an instant at the hand with which I had beaten him and there was no trace of the visual proof of his mortality. The center of the ring glowed again with a slight red hue.

I gave in to despair and shouted their names as I crossed by empty streets. I couldn't stand there alone, waiting for them to appear for the rest of eternity. Suddenly, as if the cries and the blood had opened a very heavy door, a stream seized me. A stream of jubilation and power, which traversed all the fibers of my being. It was back. My energy was there again.

Exultantly, I jumped and kept in the air. I could not believe that I was really there, suspended in the air, enjoying again of all my nature... of everything I thought I had lost forever. I allowed myself to enjoy a moment, I just wanted a second, to go through all the fibers of my being. In the midst of all that disaster, inside me shone hope.

From that position I could see better the place where they all were. I saw all the strongest of the humans fighting a Hunter, who had strayed fatally from all others, though he seemed to be lost, surrounded by so many humans, I was not surprised when I saw them all burn. They were no match for them.

"This is where the new world begins!" I heard a familiar voice screaming. A voice that was stuck in my memories, making my rage to resurface. "Here are the creatures you moaned so much for!"

"This is not what we wanted!" Anaëlle, whom I had always seen with an immaculate appearance, now presented the vivid image of misfortune. She was a reflection of what was happening. "You never understood anything!"

I saw her in a circular square, only a few houses were separating us. A hunter pushed her against the ground with a kick. She rose and charged against him, to clash again squarely against the ground, that second time, she did not get up. Blood sprang from her nose and from her back, it seemed that a wound had reopened. I looked for the twins in the midst of all that chaos, but there was no sign of them, nor of their sister.

"I understand what's enough for a broken group!" Bayron appeared before her. He descended from the opening of the roof, floating as if it were fog what fell and not desolation. My father's red cloak floated around him, marking the aura of hatred that was so much typical of him. "Those who are satisfied with the word of a demon," he continued to say, drawing a dagger from his waist, "do not deserve to know the truth. We could have had it all," his eyes were lost in a memory. "But you insisted on worshipping a chimera! You deserve not achieve greatness!"

"The closer you are to that greatness," Anaëlle rose, the shreds of her dress floated around, protecting the flesh that was uncovered, "the more you will sink in a well of despair! Your search will never end! You will only leave pain and death at your step! That's the only thing you'll achieve."

Bayron's face, distorted by wrath, shrank into a grimace while sinking the dagger into Anaëlle's chest. The blood sprang from the wound, a crimson spring that fed the soil with a life. All of them were lost in the research of something they did not understand, even she, who said in her last words that no one would be able to get to have it, spent the last hours of her life bluffing at us to achieve it. Bayron had massacred those who were once his family, and why? Due to the promise to attain something greater... the vision of being something else. The empty words of someone powerful and sick, a creature from another world who stabbed a poisoned dagger in their souls, telling them it was a rose.

The wind moved my hair and brought me her scent. I saw her watching the scene too, sitting on the edge of one of the houses, as if nothing that happened had to do with her. I approached, fearing that she would tell me that Bruce or Bob were wounded or dead and what I saw surprised me. Her white sweater was stained with blood and the trousers had as many stains and holes as the robe with which she got there.

"Hec...!" I stopped myself, seeing the corpse resting on her back. It was a Hunter, a poor dreamer who had dared attack the only creature that, in total certainty, none could hurt. Still, I was surprised. "What...?"

She shrugged her shoulders.

The armor created her an excessively sturdy body and still dead, she was surrounded by an aura of strong power. I wanted to approach to help his energy to find the way. I withdrew the helmet from her head and posed it without too much delicacy on the floor. The armor was worth nothing without energy that gave it life, it was dying next to the Hunter. That woman's immaculate face made me think of my mother. Maybe she looked that quiet now that nothing disturbed her. I passed my hand through her hair and cheek, feeling what was left of her, freeing herself and ascending to a level for which I still had no key.

"Hey!" I cried out, feeling Bayron's gaze upon us. I had to arouse her interest before he came. "Listen!" I took her vehemently on both shoulders. "Bayron can die! I had touched his blood!" I showed her the hand of the ring, even though there was no sign of it no more.

It took a few seconds, but that statement made her blink.

"That's…" She seemed frightened. She caged my hand with his. "Take it off! Take it off!"

"Stop! Oh! Didn't you understand what I had said?"

We struggled around that corpse. I knew that Bayron was approaching us, but I had to focus on not losing my balance, and my hand. I didn't have much time to assimilate what was happening to her or even what she was referring to. "Take it off! Take it off!" That was all she said. In none of our melee encounters I had seen her so determined. She always seemed to be somewhere else but, that time, absolutely her whole mind was focusing on that idea. "Take it off!"

"No!" Roared Bob, approaching us. I lost my balance, possibly because of his intervention and Hecate's persistence.

In the fall, I put my free arm between the ground and me, to be able to get up more quickly when she fell on me. Although something put an end to that dispute: a beam of white energy struck squarely against Hecate's body. It even burnt some of the hair that stood in its way.

"No!" Bob repeated, totally out of himself.

He passed by my side like an exhalation. He ran without thinking, simply letting himself be carried away by the fire that ignited his brain. I do not know if he was able to hear what I said to her or if simply the pain due to the loss dominated the situation. Bob ran, naively, to avenge her, dominated by a feeling that I did not know. He set foot on the edge in which she had sat moments before and pounced on Bayron. He didn't even make the hint to turn away, he just let him pounce into the void. He raised a hand and froze him at that instant.

"Don't do it!" I found myself begging.

His yellow eyes shone. He moved his fingers around Bob's body, who released his last words. A few words that pierced his soul, until they reached Hecate's ears. She threw her energy very late. The blow that she wanted to give Bayron, remained as a desperate attempt, a frozen movement with which she ended up collecting the blood that used to circulate through her partner's body. So many years fighting against life to stay together and that's where it all ended.

Our existence stopped at that instant, which lasted until it became a lifetime. A life full of horror and blood, in which there was no room for anything that emitted light or hope. Hecate fell on her knees to the ground, trying in vain to collect what was left of Bob. I ran clumsily towards her, not knowing very well what it was I should do or say. I passed my arms by her back, that time if he were to shoot at us again, I would block the blow.

"No, no, no..." she mumbled, embracing the blood that covered her. "No, no, no."

"Look at..." he said, wearing a smile that covered his whole face, "what mankind has reduced you to," his feet touched the ground and the cloak got stuck to his body. "Before," he raised his arms, to make his words stronger, "two great goddesses. Now, two poor rats waiting for their end," he stood still a few meters away from us. I was trying to find some way out, but I couldn't leave her there, broken as she was. A part of me was struggling to abandon her and the other one for staying. "Bring the pet!"

"Bruce!" I mumbled, pressing Hecate's shoulders tightly.

Two Hunters appeared in the smoke of the rubble, each holding one of his arms, making him look like a doll about to break. The hair hid his face, his heartbeat stuck in my ears, he was really striving to stay conscious. Our looks found each other when they placed him right where Bob had died. I lived once more, in just a second, the barbarity that had committed Bayron and before the fear of making it real, I got up as moved by a spring.

"Stop it! No, don't do it!" I ordered. "You win!" Those words lacerated my throat. "Put an end to all this and..." my voice faltered, "and I will go with you!"

A laugher came from his lips. He jumped and fell back suspended in the air, allowed himself the luxury of spinning several turns on himself, while laughing.

"No!" Bruce began to kick. "Don't do it! He's going to kill us all anyway!"

"Yes!" The greatness of a murderer is lost for a child!" They pushed Bruce to the ground, he could barely protect his head in the blow. "They're not that strong! They do not possess the power that they so bragged about! We can't believe in such weak beings!" He pointed at Hecate, who continued mourning Bob's loss. "There is no power in someone who surrenders!"

Bruce crawled all the way to where we were. I bended over again, wanting to protect them both. Really hoping that with that, it would all be over already.

"Take a good look at each other!" his tone was hardened as he added, "It really enervates me that you to feel something..."

The Hunters were carrying the rest of the humans, what was left of their old community, of their old family. There were not too many, there was no problem to leave them all in a visible place. Most of them looked at Bayron with a mixture of fear and admiration. Maybe he was fulfilling the dream of many of them. I saw Monique take her hand to her mouth, I saw her tears spurt out when she found the lifeless body of her sister. Only she and one of the twins dared to break the circle in which they had been left.

"Our first agreement is nullified," he moved his fingers in the air, as if it were a game. "Let's say that... it has been disintegrated," he released another laughter. "She is useless for me, now," he continued, looking at Hecate. "And I don't want Ribek to be distracted by the ideas of his filthy brother. It is difficult to find qualified humans..."

"Bruce," I said, lovingly, "don't let them turn your light off."

"Don't say goodbye!" He shouted, in tears. He jumped into my arms and hugged me tight, like never before. "Don't go..."

I tried hard to remember every detail of his body and his voice, I never wanted to forget him. All the moments that I had shared at his side, no doubt, had been wonderful.

"I'll never forget the name you gave me," I passed a hand through his face. "I won't forget any of the moments you gave me."

Hecate pushed us as she got up. Her rage fell upon us like a waterfall. Because of the moans I heard below, I knew they felt it too. Suddenly, as if the sun had come down to light the room, she acquired a supernatural radiance. Her body, covered with Bob's blood, the only thing that kept her tied to sanity, she suffered several convulsions until being surrounded by a black aura. A poisonous energy that would soon harm us. She raised an arm, leaving Bayron and the Hunters prey of her power.

"Allow me a moment with it," she said to me, with a sweetness I had not heard in a long time.

She directed her other arm to my breast. She didn't even touch me, but I felt that she was ripping something off me. It didn't seem to be against my will, because whatever it was that she was taking away from me, it was gushing out of my interior. She opened a well that I kept closed and she took everything she wanted. My field of vision was shrinking as that energy came out of my body. The smoke, the fire and all the cries, gathered and went through me, to make me fall to a purple hole, as purple as the Hunters. Bruce's arms were what stopped my fall; for a moment I saw Hecate, surrounded by mustard-colored fire, in the part that was closer to her body, and by the blackest mist that I had seen, as it moved away from her.

"No! No!" Howled Bayron. "No! No!"

"What good is immortality to me..." inquired, with an expression of serenity in her face that I had only seen in her sculpture, "if I cannot share it?"

That's the last image that I managed to distinguish that night. After that I received an excruciating pain. A stream that lacerated my arm and kept it twitching for hours. Tiny currents crossed my brain and ended up in my arm, contributing to the terrible pain that I felt. I opened my eyes, to see what was it that was producing it and I found myself in a dark and cold limbo. A place where the calm reigned put my pain at ease and transported me through a myriad of bright colors, some colors that made me feel new, as if there had never been any pain, no problem. A really beautiful place, where I only felt love.

However, that feeling which seemed to be lasting a lifetime, ended as soon as my back hit the ground. I felt the pain spread to my neck and legs, but when I opened my eyes and saw Bruce well, nothing else mattered.

"Bruce..."

"You are here..." he whispered, opening his eyes.

We heard a series of lamentations and we were able to verify that the rest of humans were also with us, including Anaëlle's body, to which Monique continued to embrace.

The place we were in was burned. It seemed that something had been burning for days, for the earth's condition was as black as the aura that covered Hecate. Thinking about her made me take a leap, I wanted to check that she was okay. I didn't see her anywhere.

"Ha!" Someone who walked towards us, exclaimed, with an attitude as paused and curious. "I was looking for a meteorite and...!" She was a dark-haired woman, wearing a red coat that hid her body.

The force that she was giving off was incredible. Her words stopped when our eyes met. I hoped I wouldn't have to fight at that moment, I really felt tired and didn't even know why.

"Where are we?" Monique asked, too vehemently.

The stranger opened her eyes, amused at her question.

"The questions," I tried to remember the last thing that had happened, "I ask them."

Monique receded a few steps, intimidated. I took my hands to my head. After all I had seen, my energy was badly exhausted. Where was Hecate? Where all of us were? Where were Bayron and the Hunters?

"Oh, God...!" One of the humans interrupted. Someone who seemed to be one step ahead of others. "I know where we are..." he whispered, fearing what his next words would be. The amusement that that stranger felt was on the rise. "We're in Spain."

They all murmured something. It seemed like Bruce and I were the only ones who didn't understand what was going on.

"That's right, Baby Einstein!" Granted the woman, putting her hands in her pockets. A gust of cold air struck us, I knew from the way they all shrug on themselves. "This is the place where it all started. The place where all things begin," she added, noticing how Bruce and I held hands.

Epilogue

«The Worst Nightmare»

We walked all the way to the foot of some mountains. That mysterious woman urged us to follow her and being in our situation, we did not replicate. I let myself be dragged through a very long and slightly steep staircase, which made it really easy to walk.

We went through several doors, several controls. Many people who watched us with curiosity and... Fear. Wherever I looked, even in the midst of my stun, I saw the fear in their eyes. I closed mine and allowed myself to continue.

"She's the one who got us out of there," I heard someone say. "She saved us."

Days later, after getting lost on a repair trip, I explored the place next to Bruce, although I have to say that he had already done it. It was a group of humans much larger than Monique's, much better organized and... At least on the surface, they seemed much more stable.

Each morning they met in different places to train their bodies and minds. They had accepted Bruce without any problems, except when I approached. Humans dissolve like fish when a shark approaches.

I knew the people who controlled what was happening there. I got slightly surprised to see that woman in the thick coat between them. She smiled broadly when she heard my story, in which I did not include any crucial detail, I had already made that mistake many times.

"You can stay here as long as you wish," she told me, she had a warm and very big smile. "We don't want anything from the Nephilims. We just want to live in peace."

Most humans shared a room where they slept and performed most of their daily activities. Except for a small number of compartments, away from all that racket, in which only the most important members were staying, besides Bruce and me. They said it was a reward for my great feat to get them all out of there, but I knew it was because everyone was afraid.

Despite knowing that we were out of danger, Bruce and I slept together, I lost consciousness at the bottom of his eyes and also I let he be lost in the depths of mine; when our hands were joined there was no temperature difference, that was my perfect place.

Why Hecate had sent us there? I tried to understand, however, we had several days there and my memories were extinguished as soon as Hecate's words came out of her mouth. From there on, there was nothing.

There was a day when I felt that my energy was back to a high level, we could soon leave to adjust accounts with Bayron. I smiled too fast because, almost instantly, my armor diluted completely, like a puddle of ink crashing into the ground.

"No!" I cried, desperate. "Come back!" I pounced on it, trying to put it back on my body, but it slipped through my fingers until it disappeared.

Without the protection of the mineral, I felt the breeze as a blow and the vision of my body made me shudder. My arm was black, from the elbow to the fingertips, the only thing that kept its original color was the red stone of the ring, which seemed to curl up like a snake. I moved my fingers, fearing they'd be disabled.

I felt the need to run to the mirror in the room. I had to see what it looked like. The tousled hair made my face softer than it really was, but the first thing that caught my attention was the two sapphires from the center of the mirror. I blinked, believing that thus it all would fade away. I opened my eyes and ran with my burned hand the hole in my neck.

That's what happened to a body that used too much energy. Now I knew, it was the only chance. Hecate took part of me, to form a larger vessel that would get us out of there. If my forearm offered that look, she was probably dead. It was the price for taking more...

Almost instantly, a cramp gripped my belly, an acute pain that made me bend over myself and contain a shout. I tried to get to the bathroom, but I collapsed on the table, causing the jars and boxes to rush to the floor. I took a hand to the belly, as if that would soothe the pain. Something warm slipped through my thighs, I introduced my hand between them and the vision of that reality, confirmed all my fears.

If you bleed, you can die.

Acknowledgements.

I hope this story has captivated you, just as it captivated me. It is my first novel and as such it has a great sentimental value, as well as that you have reached this last page.

I could not have finished writing it without the support of my friends, among whom I have a fabulous artist, who took care of the cover; of my family, who endured what is not written in the writing process; and of course, I couldn't have finished it without you. Without you, reader, this would not be more than empty pages full of lettering, you have brought the magic.... The energy that makes battles possible and keeps us connected in the universe. I hope to have that power in the next part of the story and all that are to come.